Evincepub
Publishing

Published by

Evincepub Publishing

Shivam Complex, Bilaspur, Chhattisgarh 495009
Ph.: +91-9171810321
e-Mail: publish@evincepub.com
Website: www.evincepub.com

First Edition: 2023
ISBN: 978-93-5673-184-4
Publication Month: January

SIZZLING

with...

SHE 2 SHE

Strictly for 18+

By

Shaheen Kazi

ABOUT AUTHOR

"From Nothing
To
Something"

Shaheen Kazi is an Indian Author; being from Mumbai. She settled in Gulf (Saudi Arabia) for more than two decades. After perusing IATA, she focused on her passion for writing. Her achievements include six books, three anthologies, and many forthcoming projects. She is a versatile author. She also writes short articles for *The Literature Times*. Sometimes for a change, she works as a Reviewer at *MouthShut.com*. Her books are always picked by readers from any Bookfairs.

If you think writing is only her passion so am sorry to let you know that she is also a reader. She loves reading books by other authors too. Books have always been her best friend. Libraries and Bookstores have always fascinated her from a younger age. In this digital world, mobiles are essential, but according to her, books are the best place to live. She is a non-kindle reader and can never read any book on Kindle. Yet, she never travels without her book. Her journey was not so easy, but her belief was strong.

She firmly believes in being somebody when nobody thought you could be.

Besides writing, she loves reading, travelling, knitting, painting and singing. She is excellent in her culinary skills too. But, as a mother, her son will always be her prime priority.

Her belief is,

"Authors Write
but
Readers Complete".

CONTENT

FROM THE AUTHOR'S DESK

I guess you're wondering what I wrote instead of a romance novel. "Lesbian," what are your thoughts when you think of that word? Be honest. If I'm not mistaken, your mind gets nasty and reminds you of sex. If you have sex in your head, you can't blame yourself. Because films or novels without sex do not arouse the audience and the reader.

Lesbianism is their way of making love with their choice of partner, but judging them for *sex* simply because they are lesbians, is not suitable.

You must have read multiple erotic fiction, erotic books or articles. But writing about lesbians wasn't the easiest thing for me. I could have easily written something about the man and woman's secret affairs, but intentionally I did not pen it down in volume 2 after writing Sizzling With Next Volume 1.

Readers of Volume 1 knew what that book was all about.

The answer is that we sometimes ignore them *(very special people)* intentionally. Being lesbian/gay/bisexual or transgender (LGBT) is not a crime.

They're also human, and they have feelings like us. Of course, their preference differs from ours, but that does not make them taboo or comical characters in society.

First of all, we all need to understand lesbianism. Lesbians look like women and have their month-to-month cycle like all women. Like every other woman, she also cares for her skin, beauty and fashion. She is also physically feminine. It's all the same, so why is she known as a lesbian? Yeah, everything's the same, but her sexual preference differs from regular women's. Her sexual interest makes her unique compared to the average female group.

The world is composed of various thoughts, behaviours and preferences. However, everyone needs two factors: Acceptance and Respect. But unfortunately, some young people under the lesbian category are afraid to reveal their sexuality to their family or close friends. Why? Think of that question.

Fear. Fear arises at the first stage, and then from fear, rejection is encouraged. Indeed, fear is their most important enemy. They are afraid of opening up and talking because they cannot trust other people. As a result, they feel uncomfortable sharing their truth with their family or close friends.

Rejection. In every stage, when their bucket is filled with fear and lack of confidence, rejection always remains in their mind. They are afraid to be shunned by society, family and close friends. What will happen if someone finds out? No one would love to be my friend, particularly girls and women. So what are they supposed to do? Should they stop living life, stop stepping out of their zone and should stop breathing?

"Sizzling With . . . She 2 She" has ten different stories about Lesbians. On each level, you will be able to understand and may connect with their sentiments. Of course, not many women aren't born lesbians, but sometimes something changes in them, and they decide who they will be only for their excellence. Concealing their realities from families and society cannot be easy for them; how they overcome so many obstacles and want to be accepted by their loved ones.

In this book, you can even go through some stories that few women were born, unlike lesbians. But, due to unavoidable circumstances in their lives, they choose to love someone of the same gender. Love does not have a gender; it is a sense of an invisible chain that connects the soul. Joining the right person means everything. Acceptance and comprehension are the only two keys they need from ordinary people like me and you who live in this normal society with them. In every story, you will understand the journey of every woman that has happened in their life.

Read their narratives in their voices; you will sense them.

After reading this book, if you encounter LGBT people in your life, show respect and humility to them instead of intimidating them. At times, a small positive gesture can make all the difference.

Finally, I would like to end by saying that we all need equal respect. Thus, if you are not LGBT, thank God and be a good person for your thoughts and actions. And if you are LGBT, don't get upset; be proud of yourself because God has special care and love for you.

LGBT people do not need sympathy; they need empathy. Is it so a big thing to offer?

SHAHEEN KAZI

Sometimes the quest ends with the same gender

Online Friendship

June was full of the rainy season and meant nothing to me. Since I was born in April, my grandma retained my name April. I was looking for employment, but my stars were not in my favour. I was going through some rough times in my life back then. My destiny was also not supportive of my career and my personal life. One lazy Sunday evening, I was alone at home, searching for movies after reading a thriller book. All my friends enjoyed their romantic weekend with their sweet friends, and I was not in the mood to be with anybody. While searching for good movies on Netflix, I received a friend request from an unknown messenger on my mobile.

Months before that, I broke up with my boyfriend, Tom. That was my sixth breakup, and I was tired of being dumped. I had therefore decided that I would not fall back into love traps. My relationships have never been more than a year long. Whenever I took my relationship further, something or another would become a massive problem.

I have never been pleased in my previous relationships, some played with my emotions, and some deceived me. So, after my last breakup, I decided to stop chasing romance. After getting dumped a sixth time, I realized love is a fantastic feeling; cheap lovers like my *ex* can never understand the depth and beauty of love. And if I ever want to go ahead with someone, I will not be in a hurry to donate my heart. Sometimes breakdowns make you realize it is better to be alone than stay with the wrong person.

After surfing the Netflix movies list for ten minutes, I turned off the television. Then, I grabbed my phone and accepted the request of the unknown friend. And the reason was that somewhere I loved that cute teddy bear photo which was visible on display.

Within a few minutes, somebody launched a message in my inbox. The sender's identity was A.D.

What kind of name is it? I wondered. I checked that A.D. profile to see the person, but I only found some photos and videos of nature, wildlife, animals and birds in the gallery. So, I raised my head and took a shot at finding an intelligent new friend. I thought to start chatting with A.D.; after seeing his photography collections, it was easy to understand that he must be a nature lover or a photographer. And if he is a nature lover, he must be someone good with whom I can be in the friendship zone. And if he is a photographer, so he understands natural beauty, I can even learn some photographic skills from him and think about my career. So, in both cases, my friendship with A.D. can become fascinating and adventuresome.

A few moments later, A.D. sent me the message again, and we started to chat. I was not curious to know who A.D. was because I felt better sending and receiving texts somewhere. It was an excellent little informal conversation on the first day. That evening, we sent each other goodnight messages and promised to meet again online.

Days went by, a month went by, and somewhere my days of depression went by too. I found employment in a library as a librarian. So, spending the day in the library was an antidote to my mood; surrounded by many terrific books, I began to feel calm. The vibrations of the books were like self-help to my soul. In my spare time, I read good books of various kinds. Bit by bit, I began a new life and a new way of thinking. I was holding no grudges for none of my ex-lovers, I felt lighter, and somewhere I had forgiven all my ex-nerds.

One night, I came home early. That night, I was extremely excited about my first salary. I was in an upbeat mood, and I wanted to celebrate. So, I opened food apps on my phone and searched for pizza menus to give myself a calorie-rich treat. While enjoying my pizza on the bed, A.D.'s message dropped on my phone. I was delighted to see A.D.'s words after two months. I shared with A.D. my work and the positive change in my life. A.D. was a very humble person and was incredibly happy for me. We again started chatting with each other. A.D. had been out of town for a few months and was working on a wildlife project. He visited distinct parts of Africa to gather raw images of wild animals. A.D. shared some of their photo collections with me as well. From his click, my guess was correct. He was a photographer. But I had not seen him so far, and I did not want to. I was comfortable without seeing him and chatting. Sometimes you can chat with a stranger more comfortably, even not knowing what they look like, because after looking at the faces, your brain starts judging, and your innocent heart starts expecting. Being alone for so many months and reading so many books, I have always sounded like a philosopher to myself. Secondary effects, I suppose!

Gradually, we both started chatting again in the night. I have shared all my breakup stories, feelings, and everything with A.D. And patiently, A.D. has always been online without passing judgment or interference. A.D. always allowed me to type how much I wanted, and after my text, he answered me without missing even one of my texts. I found a lovely friend in A.D. And A.D., too, was quite comfortable with me sharing all his daily nature of work. The beauty of our relationship was that neither of us was curious about the other. However, we were developing understanding and affection for each other. We did not even share our contact number; our meeting place was fixed online.

One evening, we decided to switch our friendship from the digital world to the real world. So, we planned to meet in a restaurant for dinner. We were both looking forward to meeting at the end of the week.

Saturday night . . .

In the frosty winter of December, I got to the restaurant. I was so excited to meet him that it made me walk half an hour earlier. I made reservations for both of us. My heart was beating at supersonic speed as the thoughts of meeting my online friend for the first time were personal. A lot of curiosity was running inside me, like how he must be looking? What will be his reaction after seeing me? He, too, must be excited, like me, to see me in person. I was shivering about questions and thoughts running through my mind then. For this meeting, I even bought a new dress to impress A.D.; well, the new dress cost me a little too much. Still, as it is always said, *'The first impression is your last impression,'* and somewhere, I do not want to make our evening sound boring or leave any unimpressed impression of meeting on A.D. Every minute went by like an hour to me.

After waiting fifteen minutes, I received an A.D. message.

'Hello, where are you? I already reached.'

My heart began to pounce like a hammer, and I was sweating out of excitement. In my mind, I was practising the rehearsal to meet and greet what I had practised before leaving the house.

So, I immediately typed the message, *'I'm waiting at table number 5.'*

After sending my message one last time, I checked myself by picking up the teaspoon near me to ensure that my nervousness did not ruin my hair and make-up. My eyes were fixed on the doorway with a great smile on my lips.

In the meantime, I heard a gentle feminine voice, "Hello, April,"

I looked at her with strange expressions.

Again she said, "It's me, darling . . . your friend A.D."

When I listened to this friendly tone, I turned my head from the entrance toward her. A tall, beautiful, thirty-year-old woman with thick, gorgeous black hair stood before me. I stood up and greeted her, not in the way that I had rehearsed, of course. She had a friendly smile and a lovely silhouette. She walked up to me and hugged me warmly. When she put her arms around me, her hair smelled of vanilla. The scent of her shampoo gave me a meaningful boost of positivity and happiness. And I was so surprised that in the last two months I was chatting with a woman, SHE was not HE. She was the person with whom I shared all my daily worries and activities at night.

She introduced herself as Alexa Dan, and quite comfortably, she sat on the chair beside me. Nevertheless, I did not want to express my shock, so I sat beside her. We ordered something to eat and drink. To my surprise, she also loves to drink gin with lemonade. The glasses made us talk more. She was a woman of total control, and I started to like her more personally. Her posture and her sharp features were imposing. When I spoke to her, I noticed that she was a good listener; she was always attentive while listening to me without being absent-minded. We both had a wonderful dinner together, and it was a bit of a disappointment that A.D. was Alexa, not Alex. *Lol!!*

After dinner, she invited me to her house. It was near the restaurant. It was a beautiful moon night. With an attractive person, how could I ignore the invite? So, I agreed, and we both walked the path into our mood of laughter and enjoyment. Earlier, I had never experienced such a romantic and joyful December evening. The sky was clear, and there was a holiday season all over the place. Alexa and I padded and smiled at each other regularly like we were experiencing the same emotions. It was a magical walk that just two lovers could feel.

Once I got to Alexa's apartment, I felt comfortable. Alexa was staying alone with her luxurious things. Her daring fine paintings were the most elegant masterpiece in her living room. When I was looking at her photos, she came to me with a glass of gin and soda. When she walked into the room, her sculptural frame was so slim and beautiful, and her long dark hair was loosely held back with a decorative clamp; it was breathtaking. Now I had begun to appreciate her company even more, and having a drink with her was a big moment. The beautiful pictures clicked by it were breathtaking frames to marvel at! Alexa was not only a beautiful woman, but she was exceptionally talented and intelligent as well.

While we were drinking, our eyes ran into each other, and something we both felt simultaneously. We looked at each other in silence as though our spirits were connecting. Alexa took the glass from my hand and drew near me with her gentle hands; she touched my face with her long, beautiful fingers and progressively moved her long, manicured fingers across my lips. She felt my hair and sniffed it. A chill filled my spine, and I began to love her touch. She placed her bright and sexy lips on my neck; her soft lips were on my skin, overshadowing all my senses and control of my body. I squeezed her around her waist, and for a minute, our eyes saw each other again, and we began to caress each other passionately. We were so absorbed by one another that we did not even understand that we had reached the bedroom. She took my clothes off and started kissing my whole body. I was lying on her bed, NAKED. She slowly took her clothes off one at a time. Finally, my eyes were on her sexy body, she got out of her leather pants and her long-sleeved sweater, and I said in my head, *'She's fucking hot!* Then she kicked her boots and was soon in her lace push-up bra and a matching G-string, which made her even sexier than before. When Alexa was out of her clothes, I got aroused to see her curvy voluptuous body. Her breasts were round and heavy, and she also had gorgeous round buttocks. I was lying on the bed, and she was grinning as she slowly made her way to the bed. It looked as if she was hovering above the carpet rather than walking. Alexa hooked her fingers in her thong and tore it out. The nipples looked at me with a welcoming look, as if they were waving to somebody to suck them. As Alexa reached the edge of the bed, she placed her hands between my separated feet and crawled gently between my legs. As her sexy cherry lips met mine, she squeezed into me; her fingers seized my short blond hair and pulled my face towards her.

My hands then dragged towards her boobs, which were clenched in mine. I squeezed each one and worked my hands towards her already hard nipples. Her pelvis was resting against mine, forcing my legs to spread as far as I could. I moved my groin to get a little friction, but she cambered her back away as she kept kissing. Eventually, she came to me, and we slid under the bedspreads. Her kisses were full of seduction, and her long fingers within me were no less than any tough masculine adulthood. She pushed herself far enough to push a small hand on my body to my bosom and rolled the nipple between my finger and thumb breaking our kiss to get it into her mouth. I gasped as she nibbled it gently before moving back down my body the way she had come.

I never intended to have sex with a woman. Once I had Google: 'How to have sex with a woman if you are a woman.' I never thought in my life that one day the time would come when I'd be having sex with a woman.

That whole night we made love to each other. We have explored each other and opened our hearts and souls without hesitation. I never felt better and more complete in my last relationship with those men than I had with Alexa that night. She gave me everything—her trust, her sincerity of love, and her company, which was only for me. That was the first time I had a relationship with a woman.

Until now, we had no regrets about what we had done. It is not that we were lesbians from the moment we were born. In every woman, there is a beautiful woman who lives in herself. Only a reasonable person must remove her from the cage of rules and fear.

We both started as online friends from there; our fate brought us closer together. Alexa was conscious of her feelings for me and made me realize how valuable I was.

It has been six wonderful years, and we are so in love. After meeting Alexa, I never thought about finding a relationship with men, and neither did Alexa have a crush on anyone. Instead, our relationship got more asserted and beautiful. I had been given many men opportunities in my previous life but ended up with tears and unhappiness. So, I gave myself, my inner woman, a chance to be with someone like me, even if SHE is not HE.

Overall, it's a matter of my CHOICE.

Age Break

I am twenty-four, and she is forty-seven. I bet many people see us oddly after they are aware of our relationship. Our significant age gap made our relationship always 'unique' and 'special'.

When I first met Sheena during one of our pleasant evenings, I instantly fell in love with her. We were similar in various ways, although we had a significant age difference. Yet, being with each other made us unique; somehow, the positive vibrations always affected our relationships.

I remember it was a Christmas party, and I was invited to Roger's house. Roger was a perfect-looking guy, and we were also sweet childhood friends. We both grew up together. Our families always thought about us several times, but we never came to grips with each other in that way. Perhaps, Roger was the only person who had always known my dark secret that I was a lesbian. I never even tried to speak to my family about what I wanted, not because I was afraid but because I was uncomfortable speaking openly with them.

Sheena was an attractive woman in her forties and was single and happy. She scarcely looked in her forties, and I was about to ask her age, but she asked my age first. When we introduced ourselves, I gradually became acquainted with her. She used to work as a paediatric nurse. When Roger introduced me to her, I lost my heart because of her beautiful smile and expressive eyes. She was amicable and pleasant company to be around. However, after exchanging our meeting and welcoming formalities, Sheena became silent. As though she had nothing to say. But even her silence pulled me even more towards her. Somewhere I could sense that she was uncomfortable with me because of the age difference. So, I decided to be at the forefront of breaking the ice. Then, charmingly and politely, she started answering me, and in return, she started asking me some questions about myself, which was a good sign for me. As time passed, I noticed that she was getting a little more comfortable, which was vital.

While laughing and talking, I held her hand at the party and noticed she was not having a problem with it. When the dance music changed to romantic, I asked her to dance with me.

In the beginning, she laughed and said, "O dear, how can we dance to this romantic music? You should look for someone else; look around you; there are so many hot guys out here."

However, she was stuck in the age net and to make her feel more at ease without a word; I took her hand and led her to the dance floor. As we both came onto the dance floor, all the party guys in the rocking party started throwing us curious looks. I noticed from the corner of my eye that some people were continuously staring at us, but I was good enough to ignore them because my eyes were fixed only on this beautiful lady I loved. Finally, in the middle of the dance, Sheena asked me to stop as she noticed some weird eyes on her. I took her face in my hands and told her to look only into my eyes and that rest did not matter to us. And that night, our dance developed into a great connection. Even at her age, Sheena was extremely graceful with her movements. While dancing, it surprised me and made me realize even more that, being younger than her, I was somewhere not up to that mark while balancing my dance moves with her. As I saw Sheena dancing gracefully, my heart was pounding higher to hold her in my arms.

Later that evening, my heart was not in favour of leaving her, so I offered her a lift. Sincerely, giving her a ride was only an excuse to spend more time with Sheena. She happily agreed and sat with me in the car. Obviously, after having such a good time with each other, I was no longer a stranger to her. While driving, my mind was distracted whenever my eyes crossed her thighs. In the distraction, I took the wrong turn; the wrong turn was an advantage for me because I was saving additional time to spend with Sheena in the car. But there came a time when I had to say bye. With a heavy heart, when I turned towards her, I noticed her beautiful skin was flawless, and she was a woman of complete desire. When I dropped her near the gate, she gave me her contact number and asked me to be in touch with her. *'Communication with you, damn it; I only want to touch you.* I wanted to say those lines to her, but I kept my mouth shut. Like an innocent person, I smiled and nodded.

As soon as she began to walk, my eyes were fixed on Sheena's beauty, and my heart struck me from within. At that moment, I did not want to see her leave me and go into the house. I could not control myself, and I got out of the car and ran toward her. She opened the door and turned toward me.

When she saw me coming toward her, she asked, "Dear, have I forgotten anything? "

I looked into her blue eyes, which were so inviting; without thinking of anything, I kissed her. Yes, I kissed her. It was a challenging moment for me; anything might have happened. I would have been fired or punched. Although thinking about such consequences, I still initiated my actions. The situation was as if I did not express my feelings for Sheena, I would no longer be able to live in peace. And if I describe it, I might get accepted or rejected. Even if I'm thrown out, I'll live happily ever after.

Sheena was amazed by my sudden kiss attack and compelled me to leave her. But all I wanted to do was hug and tell her how much I was in love with her. At first, she felt uncomfortable with my kiss, but after a few minutes, her body language changed. She, too, started kissing me back after a few minutes. Her moist strawberry lips gave me the sweetness of honey. Our kiss absorbed us, and we went inside the house in the deep ocean of kisses. I pushed her against the wall and began kissing her neck, which I knew she would love the most. I unzipped her sexy red dress and touched her naked skin for the first time. Her skin was smooth as a soft feather. In a rapid movement of a finger, she was entirely out of her dress, standing in a black lace bra with a black lace thong. She was an absolute beauty. Seeing her in those two sexy pieces, I felt the wetness between my legs. She had perfect B-cup breasts with a slight indent in the centre of her full-toned stomach. Her breast was fully round, and it had a lovely volume. I unhooked the bra and held her cups in my hands.

"Oh my God, those are the best tits ever," I told her while kissing her.

While licking her breast, her sweet moan gave me a high of pleasure and increased my quest to drink it completely. I got my dress off, my bra off, and my panties off. I didn't shy away from using my tongue, so I licked it up to her neck and ear. When I felt that her nipples couldn't be harder, I peppered her chest with more kisses, descending lower and lower towards her centre. It provoked a blast, accompanied by her opening her legs a little for me to slip one of my own between them. She was wet, the way I was. Without thinking of anything, my hand ended up on her thighs. I poked my finger through its folds, smelling its dampness. I then drew my finger out of the love nest and carried it to my mouth, licking the cream off my finger. She tasted good, and I wanted to taste some more.

"Do you want me to lick your pussy? I can sense your warmth down there". I asked Sheena.

She was husky, and she said, "Yes."

I made her lie on the comfortable bed and started kissing her again. She quickly straddled her legs. I got on the bed and pulled her thighs apart before I lowered my head between them. I was dizzy when her feminine scent came to my head. I went down and started licking her like candy. I melted my lips on her pussy, put my tongue into the wet folds and started to run up and down the lips of the inner pussy. I let her rub her clitoris, and she moaned in pleasure. To my surprise, she had oozed out with intimacy and wetness. She was a woman with a lot of love inside her, and that love I have always needed.

After spending a beautiful night with Sheena, my eyes opened when the sun's warm, cosy rays hit my face. Unfortunately, I did not see her in the room. I could not wipe out the images of the last night I spent with Sheena. I was too sluggish to get out of bed but not finding Sheena in the room encouraged me to look for her. I could hear some sounds from the kitchen.

Another great thing I learned about her was that Sheena was an early riser. So I followed the lead of the sound. To my surprise, Sheena had prepared a beautiful breakfast with a delicious aroma next to the kitchen counter. She looked incredibly gorgeous in the daylight; I held her around her waist and snuggled my head on her shoulder. I was utterly lost in her scent and wished that time would stop forever. . . . She stopped the work and turned toward me, but I found her nervous instead of seeing love in her eyes. After a beautiful night, I asked her what was wrong and what was bothering her. She said whatever happened last night, we should forget about it and try not to repeat it in future. I was astounded because I was not ready to hear this.

I told her, "If you think it was a mistake, then you are making a big mistake by saying this. You changed my life the moment I saw you. I am in love with you, and I will not take my step back now."

After hearing me, she broke down in tears; she hugged me hard and wept a lot. She confessed that she felt my love for her the moment when I first kissed her. Sheena also constantly needed true love, but she had always left heartbroken on her love journey. And for this reason, she never liked anyone for fear of losing someone again. However, she had no courage to evade the relationship again. I assured her that nothing would happen like this when we both would be forever.

Sheena was a widow without children. After her husband's death, she isolated herself from the people around her. She met someone a year ago, but he was already married and the father of two children. And he was only playing with Sheena's emotions. He never fell in love with her. So after finding the truth, Sheena broke up with him and again led a solitary life.

Our days and nights unfold in the spirit of happiness and romance. We both thought our age gap was sexy and exciting. However, if that was not the goal of our relationship, then why were we together? We were always together because we loved each other. We were just like any other couple, and we never considered our age difference in day-to-day life.

I also introduced Sheena to my family because Sheena did not want me to share our relationship with anyone, especially in front of my family members. And even I was not in favour of revealing our relationship because I did not want my family to be prejudiced before meeting Sheena. But, somehow, she felt that my family would not accept this, and they would be in shock, and we could lose our dignity and our relationship. So, Sheena wanted me to tell my family the truth about myself, which I had been hiding for several years. She wanted me to talk to them and make them understand, and we can come at us once they know. Initially, I was not ready for this, but then I thought about it and decided to tell the truth to my family.

One night, when Roger came to my house to have dinner with his family, my parents talked about us and were very harsh about fixing the engagement date. At the table, I was surprised to hear that I did my best to speak to my mom and dad, but they were both in the mood to laugh and rejoice. Unfortunately, they set up my wedding with Roger instead of listening to me.

The commotion made me so frustrated that I yelled, "MOM! DAD . . . I'M LESBIAN!" in a loud voice.

After screaming so loud, there was silence at the table, and everyone's eyes were on me. Then, suddenly, the cheerful ambience got transformed into a silent tomb. I noticed my bold confession broadly opened Roger's mouth, and he found it difficult to make up his mind. He seemed confused about putting that delicious spoon in his mouth or keeping it on the plate in that problematic situation.

Finally, I stood up, took a deep breath, and said to the family, "I'm sorry for letting you know this about me. I can understand that this is offensive, but that is what I am. I am a lesbian with no interest in men. Roger is my best friend and always will be, but marrying a guy is not my cup of tea. So, one more time, I'm sorry."

There were still blank expressions on everyone's faces. Finally, I thought it was the right time to reveal my relationship with Sheena. That is when I closed my eyes.

Then, with all my courage, I announced, "Mom, Dad, one more thing I would like to add here. I am already in love with someone, and *She* is Sheena. My True Love and my Life."

Hearing this, my parents were shocked, and their eyes widened. Finally, my father rose angrily and ordered me to leave his house and never show him my face. I have already bought much awkward shame to my family. And after my confession, staying with them was out of the question. My mother cried without any inhibitions.

Roger gave me the hand of friendship. He asked me to stay with him in his house as he had no one to share his room with, merely I denied it and thanked him for the offer because my destination was with Sheena and nobody else.

****

It has been five years, and I am staying with Sheena happily. Sometimes when we spend time together, people ask us if we are mother and daughter. Frankly, they think that, but we do not mind because it is an innocent mistake. They apologize profusely when as soon we tell them we are married. It is a typical mistake, and we do not mind; even though it can sometimes be awkward, we are completely overwhelmed.

People are only rude and judgmental online because they can quickly leave hate messages using anonymous profiles. It is always sad to hear critical things about our relationship, of course, but we know our love is sincere and beautiful, and we know we are not doing anything wrong or harming anyone. So, we are always prepared to face the delicate situation and the judgments of others. But to be honest, it is worth it when you genuinely love somebody.

I recall the first morning when Sheena told me about her life. I had assured her that nothing wrong would happen now. Yes, sometimes she gets anxious about me, but that is normal. In our relationship, she was concerned about our age difference; to me, age is just a number, and now for Sheena, her *'Age . . . Was Just a Number.*

The Lesbo Club

The two of us met at the Lesbo Club in September 2012. This Lesbo Club was the club of many lesbians like us, and I have been a member of that club for four years. Many lesbians, too, were a member of this club. It was not only a club for us; it was like a normal society. At this Lesbo club, we Lesbains had created our world for us. I met a lot of lesbians at that club. And whenever I visit this club, I somehow feel that in this world of ordinary people, the proportion of lesbians is growing daily, month by month and year by year.

It was pervasive to meet lesbians in that club, a lesbo club—with the same humans and feelings. The Lesbo Club was more than a home for all lesbians; however, there was no one to judge us or give us a strange look in this club. In this club, there was a great scope to meet new lesbians and to create our beautiful stories. And one day, this happened when my story started as well.

****

We were both from Manhattan, New York, and of similar age. Many lesbians found their partners in that lesbo club, and some single lesbians like me were still looking to be with somebody. So, every day after work, it was my usual routine to visit this club and have a few drinks.

One weekend, I was a little drunk that night because I had a breakup with one of my girlfriends; I was devastated. So, I was alone in the bar when a friend of mine went to see another girl she liked. It was a great evening. I recall pole dancing when a dancer took me on stage during my drinks. Since my mood was so dull, I began to feel somewhat pleasant. In the meantime, another Spanish girl crossed the dance floor and began to move with the other dancer and me. I started to feel good when the tanned bodies of the two dancers rubbed against mine. I was wholly sandwiched between a pair of naked dancers. Their arms wrapped around me, and to my surprise, one girl started kissing me all over. This seduction on the dance floor between the three of us—being kissed by two magnificent Spanish ladies was paradise. That kind of sexy dancing was a regular feature of this club, but it was my first participation.

A confession - I frugally enjoyed it. The entire blame is on my drinks.

After the dance, I returned to my former seat and continued with my glasses. Nancy noticed me and came to me first. She began to speak to me, and we both had friendly conversations for about thirty minutes. At the end of our discussions, Nancy took leave as she was in the club with one of her friends; they both were rushing to go to someone's party. Before she left, we followed each other on Instagram. So funny; I could have gotten her phone number, but this thought struck me after she left.

We followed each other on Instagram for a few months and would love to see each additional photograph, but we did not start talking again until 2013. I remember it was one of my usual evenings driving home. To my surprise, I couldn't stop blushing when I noticed Nancy's comments on one of my posts. And at that moment, I decided I would message her back. That single message from Nancy was a life-changing moment for me. My fate took a beautiful turn in my void life. From then on, Nancy started responding to my message with many heart emoticons. And from her messages, it was easy to understand she was too delighted to see my message. We immediately put together a night to go on a date without wasting more days.

It was a Saturday evening. I was waiting for Nancy at a bar when she came in a glamorous black sexy dress. Seeing her coming, my heart was blasting like a bomb, and my desires were aroused. Finally, she came and held me, and I got lost in her scent. She looked more beautiful than last time. Even after a lengthy gap, the magic of connectivity was alive and well among us. There was no discomfort, no vacillation, nothing. It seemed like those two broken wires were reconnected. We always have something magical with each other. We both had a wonderful evening and spent a couple of hours together. In the meantime, she was staring into my eyes and holding my hand. Being of the same gender, holding hands in public was not a problem. People always took us as friends whenever we hugged or sat close to each other. But my heart was urging me to kiss those luscious red lips that evening. So, I asked Nancy whether she would come to my apartment.

She smiled and winked at me, swallowed her drink in one fell swoop and said, "Let us go."

It was as if she was waiting for this moment. I gulped my drink, and the two of us left the bar. On the way, she touched me with her soft hands and moved her hands on my hips. Somewhere I think she was also swimming in that same pool with me of love and desires. It was the first time I felt the distance to my home was too long. Nancy was a hot chick, and I wanted to hold her and touch her. I fell in love with her so much.

Upon arriving at my apartment, I received a professional call, which I was supposed to answer. I told Nancy to feel at home, and I'll catch up with her after the call. She shook her head with a smile and became comfortable. Every time I talked, my eyes were on her.

When I was admiring those juicy red lips, I thought, *"those pretty red lips would look damn good on my nipples."*

Nancy took off her black heels and sat on the sofa. Her legs were smooth and welcoming. There was a bookshelf near my couch, so Nancy pulled out one book. She seated herself with the book and opened it on her lap. Nancy slowly started scanning the book, looking at the photos one page at a time. At times, she would gently bite her lower lip while reading. And I noticed her long legs, crossed at her ankles, sometimes moving as if Nancy were squeezing her thighs together. I looked at her more than I responded to the call, and she was aware of this. That became a seductive game between us. She would glance up to see me looking at her, and I would smile and turn my eyes away. This continued for some time, and we were both smiling. Then, she looked at me at one point and saw that I was staring at her legs. I pondered in her eyes, but at that time, I did not look away; instead, I looked back at her legs. She looked at her book, pretending not to notice it, but turned slightly towards me. Then she stared right at me and slowly opened her legs. Thanks to her short dress, I could see her pale blue panties. My eyes focused on the spot between her thighs, and she was spreading her legs a little further. She lifted the large photo book and placed it against her waist, allowing me to see the thin lacy strip of blue panty between her legs. She turned her eyes to her book, and her legs gently and slightly rocked open and closed. I watched intently as her motion sent me signals to break all the boundaries.

After I disconnected the call, I walked to her, to a place by the shelves, and took that book in my hand. Nancy stood up, and I felt her warm breath over me.

"I was looking at that earlier. It's a beautiful book, isn't it?" I said . . . and touched her lips without wasting a moment.

Nancy took my thumb and started sucking it off seductively. Her eyes were beautiful and expressive. Her long brown hair came down on her face, which added to her beauty. I kissed her, and she kissed me back in absolute passion. Nancy began unbuttoning my blouse. She took my bra off and gave me a sense of liberty and covetousness. Her hands swept my tits, and her soft touch sent a jolt of electricity down my body to my pussy, making my clit throb with desire all the more. She was gently licking me with her sweet tongue around my nipples. I found my nipples were erect while Nancy was playing with her tongue. She groaned and was very desperate to spend every instant in profound love. I lost control of my body and enjoyed every movement myself. The night had turned magical; it was an all-night moon, and the beautiful fresh moonlight was falling on our faces. The silence of the night and milky white moonlight has enhanced the beauty of our love for one another. I pulled her down on the carpet and removed her sexy blue panty; she was utterly moist and urging me to fill her with love. I noticed that she had a clean waxed crotch, and her pussy lips were standing prominently on her thighs. She, too, had a tattoo of a butterfly just above her pussy lips, a symbol of freedom. I went down and kissed her beautiful honeypot.

Nancy's eyes were closed, and she was moaning softly, and eventually, I produced the vibrator to meet that need. When I inserted the vibrator into her tender pink pussy, Nancy jumped with excitement as she felt when the vibrator got alive in her pussy, vibrating all over her sensitive pussy walls. As the vibrator was vibrating, Nancy took me in her arms and pulled me toward her to embrace her. Nancy grabbed my hands on her breast and started rubbing it. Her lips were biting, and her eyes were closed in pleasure.

Nancy's nipples were an absolute treat for my mouth. I sucked her round breast and licked her tits to add more fuel to the fire. She enjoyed the stimulation with me by rubbing the fine edge of the vibrator on her skin. Our actions were intense . . . extremely intense . . . with seductive moans. Finally, Nancy felt the climax and shook her beautiful thighs with a flirtatious groan. Throughout the night, we kissed and felt the warmth of our naked bodies of each other. Our naked bodies were shivering under the romantic night of the moon.

After that night, Nancy and I began dating, and we have been intensely in love. After we were in love, we both ended up visiting the lesbo club. We both are not religious people at all, so our upbringing never affected our relationship. We are not the type of people who plan; we live positively in the moment. We know that no matter what, we will always be together.

Camp Fire

In February 2005, I was a high school student in London. I was single and desperate to mingle. Many good-looking guys were on my campus, but my eyes were fixed on John, the most handsome guy. John was the heartbeat of many girls during that time, and he was immensely popular for his appearance and fearless challenges. Winning numerous competitions from other universities had made John a hero in each girl's heart, including mine. John had always been an excellent, bright student and a winner in his tasks. I must have tried to talk to him a million times, but zillions of times, I failed due to my hesitations and discomfort. At some point, I was afraid of rejection. However, John was a great personality, and being with him as his girlfriend was each girl's dream on our campus.

Our school had a campfire programme for a day in Scotland, and honestly, I was extremely excited about going on this fun trip.

Finally, that morning, we were all prepared to carry our backpacks and get excited at the end of three days. The journey was behaving so well with me because John was sitting in front of me with his friends during the trip, and I was right behind him near Tina's window seat. Tina was my best friend in the class.

Amid the fun and laughter, John and I swapped looks with each other and smiled in silence. Whenever John smiled at me, my cheeks would blush, and I couldn't help but blush further. As soon as we got to the Scottish woods, we all fell in love with the beauty of Scotland. The idea of campfires in such a fantastic location was beautiful. The beauty of Scotland was in its steep, dramatic landscapes. The greenery with massive mountains and a beautiful peace refreshed our eyes and mood.

After we arrived, we all set up our tents with the help of our chosen partner. Tina was a partner of mine, and we were both involved in our activities the moment we reached the spot. John's tent was right in front of my tent, and we watched each other and felt excited while working. John was physically muscular, and watching every muscle movement while working was a feast for my eyes.

After the magnificent sunset, the evening of Scotland flowered in the group of adolescents' laughter and fun. However, few started to sing and dance around the campfire. There was music, entertainment, and food arranged by our university. It was a perfect arrangement for all of us. The evening ambience was wonderful in Scotland.

As the evening began to darken and the flames of the fire rose, the campus atmosphere turned into a happy one. John looked very handsome in his evening attire; he was wearing blue jeans and a blue t-shirt with the superman 'S' logo. My eyes were watching him all the time. I've seen a lot of guys wearing that Superman T-shirt, but that Superman T-shirt was natural justice on John's gym body. John was already taking exquisite pleasure in his band with his friends. John and I were sailing in the same boat of mischievousness; the same thoughts were running through our heads—who would first break the ice between us? I was surprised that John was also in the hesitant zone like me. Tina was playing the D.J. role, so she found some excellent music for some dances. I was sure John would pick up by somebody else, so I turned my head and started walking to my tent. To my surprise, I heard my name back there, and when I turned around, I saw John standing before me and asking me to dance with him. At that moment, I was flying over the seventh cloud, and without hesitation, I nodded to say 'yes.

When John took my hand in his hand, I felt a tingling sensation all over my body. It was the first time we had ever touched each other. Next, we started dancing together; many girls' eyes were burning in jealousy, and I enjoyed those invisible fumes. The music and bonding were growing fantastic between us. And we were getting closer and closer. Finally, John came remarkably close to me and whispered in my ear to meet him in the backyard of our campus after twenty minutes. There was nothing to hide because our feelings for one another were the same. I blushed and went along with it.

After twenty minutes,

I went into the woods to meet him and saw that John was waiting for me under the huge tree. Seeing him waiting for me, I felt he was excited for me like I was. So, I went up to him. Our eyes were encountering the same kind of desire. Without wasting any moment, John grabbed me and started to kiss me passionately. I sensed the heat in my veins as they passed through my body. I always pictured myself kissing John in my dreams a million times, but that kiss was accurate at that moment. It felt like my love star had devised a plan for me.

In the middle of our kiss, I asked John, "am I dreaming?"

He bit my neck for an answer. The pain of his bite gave me a sweet sensation in my body. Then, he took off my sweater and began touching my boobs.

From his touch, I was in an impression of his excitation motion and drowned in the atmosphere of deep intimacy. He took my clothes off in seconds, and I stood naked in front of him. John was kissing me all around my body; he slid and started to lick me while he was kissing. I was in a transitional mood and grabbed the tree's branches behind me when John began playing with my pubic hair. My breath was turning heavy, and I was craving John's adulthood. I asked John to fuck me. John hugged me tight and told me to rehearse those words.

Once again, I said, "FUCK ME, JOHN," but I yelled a bit louder this time.

After I said that, I sensed that John had stopped kissing me and moved away from me. When I felt no contact between John and my body, I opened my eyes to see him. I was shocked by what I witnessed; I saw John's friends standing before me and recording a video. I was so embarrassed, and my eyes got moist in shame. They all mocked me, including John; they all planned to have fun. John used me for fun without even thinking about my dignity. *'Fuck me'* was part of their bet. They wanted me to say these words to John. Right in front of my eyes, every boy was giving John something because he had won his challenge. Like a greedy dog, John was counting his winning amount.

I felt humiliated and helpless; meanwhile, my friend Tina came for me, covered me with a shawl, and instantly took my clothes from the ground, took me in her warm arms, and made me leave that spot. I remember I was throwing up badly; I was losing all my senses. Things were spinning in my head, and I couldn't believe what I witnessed was true. I just wanted that stuff to be a nightmare. I went back to my tent, and I started weeping hard. Tina never left the tent for a minute. All night, she stood there for me.

First thing in the morning, Tina and I decided to leave the camp and go. However, I was not brave enough to confront those boys again. With what happened last night, I was devastated, heartbroken, and shattered deep within my soul. I never expected John to pull a stunt like that on me. For me, the ugliest person on the earth was John. My love for him ended with hatred and tears. I loved John so much, but after what he did to me, he lost all my love and respect for him. Rather than love, hatred had conquered my heart.

Within three weeks,

Tina became close to my heart, and she was the one I could count on anytime without hesitation. She was a genuine, understanding friend. She helped me a lot to move on from that horrific experience. One evening, it was raining outside, and I was with Tina at her house. She asked me to stay overnight with her as she was alone that night. I was fine with it, and I agreed to be with her.

Our party started; we ordered pizza, watched scary shows, did a pillow fight, and eventually ran out and fell into bed.

After a while, Tina asked me, "Do you mind if I kiss you? "

First, I laughed, and then I turned my face towards her. She was watching me, expecting an answer. I had no idea what turned me on.

I looked into her eyes and said, "Only kiss?"

Tina smiled and stepped forward to touch my lips with her fingertips. Our lips touched slightly in the beginning, and all of a sudden, they crashed together. After that, we started kissing each other hungrily. We kissed one another deeply. Our gentle tongues touched and cherished the softness we had for one another.

Tina moved the straps down from her shoulder. She unhooked her red balcony silk bra. My fingers touched the curved part of her breast and pulled it toward me. Tina opened my blouse removed my breast from the bra, and sucked my breast with absolute passion and lust. She licked me between my two round cups holding my boobs together, giving me the hot sensationalism. And then she poured hot chocolate that was beside our bedside. A slow drip of hot chocolate touched my bare skin. Tina poured the brown chocolate on my neck, and gradually she moved her direction on my breast, my pointy tits, my waist and then my intimate area. She butchered hot, dark, thick creamy chocolate over my whole body and thighs with her soft hands. Tina began to lick with her silky tongue; the feeling of being licked was to draw billions of arrows in my veins. The beautiful passion tranquillized me at that moment, Tina sucked my breasts with a profound sensation, and she moved close to my intimate area. I had never felt that sensitivity before when Tina started playing with her tongue. Tina was perfectly aware of what she was doing with my feelings; she knew much better than I did what I wanted and deserved. I was lying on my bed, legs apart like my index finger, thumb and third finger closing around each nipple, glittering, rubbing and pulling my desire-filled ends. I was aroused beyond belief! However, my nipples were never satisfied. They did not understand the boundaries of pleasing satisfaction. I could play with them all night and desire even more. But nothing can beat the feeling of another woman's lips around my buds, sucking and shooting at my nubs to bring me to a full and fulfilling orgasm. Oh yes, girls, I am one of those lucky women who can easily enjoy some pleasant moments of rubbing tits. And I recently discovered that only a woman like Tina knows how to fulfil my desire-filled needs regarding breast play. I can never forget those lust-filled moments with Tina. Rubbing our breasts together, nipple to nipple, pulling, licking, and sucking on each other's pleasure points. I felt that my entire body was melting with desire. I was so soaked that I knew that she could feel the dampness. Tina shoved her finger in my heat zone and began rubbing on my swollen clit. A pleasant feeling filled my whole body, giving me the impression that I was going insane. Then she pressed her finger as if she knew how I felt. She moved the finger more and more quickly above my clit and then did the finger in the depths of my pleasant love slot until it was all tucked into my love nest.

While she was fucking with her fingers, she rubbed her thumb on my bud, pressing hard against the fingering, and I felt the heat begin to rise. There were sensations in my vagina. With each shot, the finger was moving faster and faster, and I was moaning in Tina's mouth harder and harder. And then it came, hard and fast. I snuggled the walls of my pussy above Tina's finger as I exploded into a massive orgasm. She fingerfucked me until my orgasm ended and took her finger out of my vagina to suck my love juice. From the look on her face, I could say that she loved the taste of my pussy cream, which made me want to taste hers. My lips smashed her mouth, and I came down to lick her pussy with pleasure. My tongue played on all her warm pussy walls, and finally, I tasted her cream. All night we enjoyed climax after climax and with one another.

That night I got my soulmate. She loved me with genuine and affectionate sentiments. Each kiss from her bound me to her soul.

So, the following day, I saw myself in full chocolate, and Tina was sleeping next to me. She looked so beautiful with the chocolate marks on her lips. I felt myself embracing her more like I did last night. But then I thought I should not disturb her sleep, so I went to the lavatory to clean myself. The moment the chilly water of the shower fell on my body, I felt as if my soul got wings of true love and sincerity. I realized that making love with Tina did not mean I was a lesbian; nobody ever gave me what Tina gave me in the relationship. She gave me her time, faith and support during my weakness, and I could escape that embarrassment only because of her ties.

I do not have good memories of that campfire night to cherish, as it was humiliating. But I can never forget how those boys treated me like a useless toy and how John threw my pure feelings in front of the whole campus. After that, I became the trending video for many days on all phones and laptops. The chuckles, the unpleasant comments, and the kind of mess I will never be able to forget.

I loved John, but John did not love me back. Tina loved me, and willingly I loved her back. I will always love her till the end. Now I need none of the men in my life to love me. Tina and my love for each other are sufficient to live a happy life.

We Are Moms

Our story is fantastic; when I (Jenny) see my eldest son, who is three years old, and the other one is on the way, in Julie's womb. I can't say enough to thank God for making my life such a good one with these angels. I had never thought that one day I would have my family.

Our story is so beautiful and exciting.

****

It was the last day of high school, where we all had fun and promised we would always be in touch. At the time, Julie was hooking up with her classmate Jimmy. I was Julie's best friend from the beginning. We were named "J3" in the class because our initial names were similar, and more importantly, the three of us were best friends. Julie was always sharing her secrets and boyfriend issues with me. I was always pleased to see Julie happiness with Jimmy. Julie and Jimmy were meant to be together because the two of them were crazy and funny. And being with them, too, sometimes I would come out of my shell and go crazy like them. I remember when we three musketeers planned to scare our teachers into the bathroom by showing them the wall with scary expressions on our faces. How were the teachers badly affected? We were such good actors that the staff began to believe our fake stories of someone standing around and watching us. As a result, the poor teachers stopped showing up in the restroom for a month.

As an orphan, I grew up in the care of my grandmother. My grandmother was a retired teacher, so I looked forward to finding a job after high school. But, to me, my grandmother was my home and my sweetheart.

After graduating, we all became very committed to our daily lives. Jimmy and Julie went to a different apartment in Los Angeles, and

I stayed back in Manhattan. I started my job at a brand store because there was good reach due to tourists. After Jimmy and Julie left Manhattan, loneliness and responsibility turned my life upside down. I used to miss them. We used to interface with each other on FaceTime all the time. In the beginning, we were in contact with one another. But as the days passed, the heavy bag of responsibilities took over our lives; our connection gradually faded following our friendship. Life is sometimes hilarious; when we are immature, all kinds of things surround us. But once you get serious in life, many things go away from your life which was the actual passkey to your happiness. Then the time came when we used to hang out and comment on social media. I saw Julie and Jimmy's pictures of travelling, dating and dining. I was glad that they were happy together. At that time, my routine was linked to work, and I was devoted to my duty. I never thought of dating someone and having some fun. I was overly attached to Julie; I did not feel that vibration with anyone else after she left. Julie and Jimmy were the only ones who made my life always full of happiness and laughter. Both were the hues of my life.

Little by little, the years passed, the time changed, and I became more mature and dedicated in my life. My grandmother, too, passed away, and after her departure, I was left to myself, no friends, no grandmother, no family; there was nothing in my life. Back then, even social media was boring for me as Julie and I had stopped commenting on each other's social status; sometimes, distances and responsibilities significantly change a person's behaviour. The equation between our J3 was also radically changed. And it happened the same thing; only the difference was that I was the only one who remained behind alone.

That is what I had in mind until I saw Jimmy in my store with a new girl one night. First, when I saw Jimmy, I could not stop and left everything on the counter, and I rushed toward him in joy. I could not control my happiness; after all, I saw him after three and a half years, and he was amazed to see me. I searched for Julie here and there. I ran outside the store to see if she was in the parking area, but I did not find her anywhere. When I came back into the store, to my surprise, Jimmy introduced me to Lucy, his fiancé. I was shocked and understood that J3 got ruined forever. I asked Jimmy about Julie, and he said he and Julie had not been dating for nine months. Things did not work out with each other, so they decided to finish the relationship and move on.

When I heard that news, my heart shattered into millions of pieces, and only one thought haunted me, where is Julie? Why hasn't she communicated with me? How can she oversee herself? There were a lot of questions that troubled me, and the only thing I wanted was to see her. My best friend needs me; that was the only thought running through my mind. So, I immediately took a week off without pay from my department and went to Los Angeles. On the way, Julie was on my mind all the time. My spirit jammed, and I desperately wanted to meet her.

When I arrived in Los Angeles, I went to Julie's house. A rusty swing and flowerpots were hanging out of her door. I pictured the time when Jimmy and Julie bought this house. At one time, they were so fond of this place and everything going on there. But their rupture had transformed the site into death. The silence had killed all the love songs and the noise of laughter.

It was early morning when I reached the spot, and I noticed that Julie's window was open; that meant she was up. I went ahead with my courage and knocked softly at her door because I did not want to startle her with a huge bang or a doorbell. I was waiting for her to open the door and surprise her. But when Julie opened the door, I was shocked to see her; she was six months pregnant. When Julie saw me, her eyes became clammy, and she held me in her arms and began to weep. Even I was unable to control my tears, and I was also draining my emotions. Finally, we saw each other after three and a half years. Julie was a completely changed woman; she was no longer that tweeting girl who was very nasty and hilarious. She held my hand and took me inside her room. The interior was good, but it looked like Julie was ignoring many things. The things that got grabbed from one place are not returned after use. I found books on the table and coffee cups by the library. Julie had spread the clothes all over the sofa; the bed sheet was wrinkled. I noticed everything at a glance, and then I saw a picture of herself and me. The photograph was beside her bed. I held the photo frame in my hand and observed Julie; she looked so happy and young in those days. I had a whole bunch of questions and a lot of complaints about her. I was angry at my friend and wanted to fight with her for not telling me about her breakup with Jimmy. Why was she suffering all alone? However, somewhere deep in my heart, I was under my control because I no longer wanted to stress her in the state of her pregnancy. Her health was my primary concern.

When Julie arrived with two coffee mugs, we sat in the lounge and started talking. The pregnancy glow was on her face, and she looked more beautiful, yet her happiness was not reaching her eyes. She was happy to see me after so long and never thought I would ever come to meet her. I told her about Jimmy and her fiancé Lucy. When she heard Jimmy's name, she cried and said that she and Jimmy were so in love that they planned to get married and move in. Things were going well in their lives until Jimmy went out for drinks with his friends and met Lucy there. And things began to change between them; Jimmy got drawn to Lucy, and even in bed while having sex, he groaned Lucy's name. Julie kept a lot of patience to give her a chance in her relationship, but things were slipping from her hands. Also, Jimmy reconsidered marrying Julie and started spending more time with Lucy. Then, one day, Julie came back home exceptionally late from work. That night was the last night of their relationship. She saw Lucy in her room making love with Jimmy, and from that moment on, Julie decided to give up on her broken relationship and asked Jimmy to leave. It seemed like Jimmy was waiting for this, and without the slightest regret, he took off. After that incident, Julie was out of her mind and decided to stay mentally strong without letting anyone know about it. Finally, after three months, she realised that she was expecting, and it was too late for an abortion.

After listening to Julie, I told her, "I wish I had known about this earlier. I would have grabbed Jimmy and taught him a good lesson".

Instead, I decided to stay with my friend, and after all this awful mess, I could not keep her in this position. So, I got the transfer and started working at the same outlet in L.A. The two of us started a new chapter in our lives. Our connection became more potent than before, and finally, that day came into our lives when our little squirrel came into our world, 'Kevin'.

Kevin is no more Jimmy's son. He is Julie and my son. Julie and I started loving each other increasingly; we both are not lesbians, but the bond between us was more robust.

It has been three and a half years; we have lived happily together. And thanks to the IVF, Julie and I are expecting another baby in our lives. I am not thinking about anybody other than Julie and my kids. Somewhere I am a man in their life. Call it fate or a coincidence, but the day I met Julie again was my chance to live with her forever.

Love has no gender; it can never be defined by conditions. True Love needs no language. It will always remain bonded by two hearts, two souls and the happiness of being together in every step of life. And we will always remain proud mothers for our kids.

She 2 She

I (Helen) have always wanted to be a painter because I enjoy sketching. I have always loved nature painting and pretty faces. But my family wanted me to be a physician, so I studied medicine because of family pressure. Although, during class sessions, my fingers never stopped drawing lines on paper whenever my eyes caught the attention of nature outside my window. Even if the pigeon was sitting on the window pane or a rainbow in the sky. My fingers always danced with the pencil. I was less interested in boys because I loved the arts. Flirting, hanging out and ending up in tears was a waste of my time. Whenever I drew pictures, I felt like I was healing the world.

When I became a science student, it was evident that science was not my tea. My future was not good in the world of science, and there was no question of being a doctor. Several times I tried to explain to my parents, but nothing happened. I finally quit explaining things to them. I thought the day they saw my results, they would get an accurate picture, and my development would make them understand that Science and I were not at all made for each other.

One lazy Monday, I was yawning in class when my eyes got the attention of a beautiful smiling face. *Ms Alice* was our new science teacher. I have never seen that beauty in any girl. When she walked into the classroom with her charming face, I got a kick out of my heart. My fingers were not in my control. I pulled out my pencils and started sketching her. I focused on the beauty more than the admiration. All my feelings were coming together. Before the end of the class, I finished her sketch, and I could not believe how my laziness turned into productivity. It was the first time when I concentrated in science class profoundly.

When we were supposed to leave our class, Ms Alice wrote something in her register as she had not noticed me for once. Only to draw her attention, I intentionally dropped her sketch near her foot and left the class.

While taking a few steps out of the classroom, "Excuse me," she said in her perfect tone.

I smiled and turned.

"Yes, you! Please come into the class right now," she said in a serious tone with a severe expression.

She raised her brow and gestured with her finger to enter the classroom. I sighed and felt sad because I thought there was not anyone in this universe to understand the arts. I went inside the course, where I found her sitting on the chair and silently gesturing for me to sit opposite her.

The class was void, and I could only hear a few sounds of paper she was turning, flicking through a few pages of her diary under the revolving ceiling fan. There was complete silence between both of us. It was the first time my eyes looked at those other dedicated students' science projects. As sketching lines on paper is art, even science is nothing less than another art form. The difference is in the arts, the artist has complete freedom of expression, and in science, the students must work in various things to do and not format. As my thoughts were engaged between the arts and science, I heard her cough gently. It was her way of getting attention. She showed me the drawing and asked why I drew her portrait in science class. I was confused when I heard her question, and I wondered if she was upset about the sketch or if she was upset about why I used her science class to make sketches.

I told her, "I am an artist, and artists are never bound by limitations. When they see beauty, they instantly add colours to it and create an exciting life. I had also confessed that I had never found a science subject so interesting, but her beauty has changed my mind today."

After I finished saying this, there was a pause between us both. Then, Ms Alice took a deep sigh and threw a gentle smile at me. She told me to meet her in the library after class. I smiled and said, "Yes, of course."

That fabulous sketch changed my life entirely. Every day after class, we used to spend time in the library. She used to help me in my studies and tried her best to make me understand several sessions of science practicals and theories. We became excellent friends, she admired my art, and I always admired her beauty silently. Our bond had become so deep that I switched from Ms Alice to Alice. Because of Alice, I started taking an interest in science and somewhere, my mind had taken a U-turn. I was changing, and more astonishingly, I was trying to be a great medical student along with my passion. At night, I would imagine her in various clothes and the next day, I would sketch her on my canvas. For me, she was like a supermodel. After that, I would send her those sketches, and she would accept them lovingly.

Finally, after spending long hours with large journals in the strange scientific laboratory decorated with skeletons and some species in the jar, Alice invited me to her house one night.

Since I was staying in the girls' hostel and Alice was away from the camp, it was not easy to come out unless I received a letter of permission from my principal. So, Alice prepared a note, and I was allowed to visit her home after classes to do additional studies. When she handed me the permission letter, she asked me to bring all my art supplies. I was highly excited for two reasons: first, to spend time with her, and second, she invited my passion. And I remember that evening, the rain was even in good spirits. It was raining at night when I hit Alice's gate. I always loved the rain, but I was upset at the wrong time of the shower. I did not want to ruin my good looks from the water above, so I took the unjust decision in a hurry. I started running and slid through the wet, sticky mud, and all my clothes were covered with dirt and soaked in water. But somehow, my artwork bag was safe. I was unpleasant because I could not turn back now and move forward into

Alice's house. But I used my logic, and after getting wet, I made the right choice. I thought it would be preferable to go to Alice's; my art supplies would be safe. I cannot afford to go back and ruin my supplies. So, I picked up my bag and knocked on Alice's door.

Alice opened the door and immediately let me into the house. First, I explained to her about the mess and how it occurred.

Then, pointing to my messy clothes, she said, "O, my dear Helen! Well, you told me otherwise; I would have thought it's your style to come home to someone like that . . ."

One thing was sure, God had blessed Alice with a charming sense of humour; she was a true example of beauty with brains.

She brought a clean towel, gave me a new pair of shorts and T-shirts, and asked me to switch. When I was changing into the bathroom, I saw her stunning collection of toiletries in the bathroom. All the expensive goodies fragranced her bathroom with lavender and roses; she was fond of beautiful costly things. Her choice made it easy to understand that Alice was an upper-class woman.

After setting her up in her living room, Alice got two hot coffees. I thanked her because, at that moment, I desperately needed it. Alice looked fantastic in her bootless pink dress. Her golden long curly hair was touching her soft shoulder. In my world of art, she was a true angel. I told her I would like to sketch her. She looked at me at length before accepting to be my muse. But it was on one condition - she wanted me to paint her nude like a Titanic movie. She wanted me to be her Jack Dawson, and she wanted to be Rose. She thought I wanted to draw her nude (I did not correct her). Alice went into her room, and I began to prepare my things; when Alice came out, I saw her standing in her silky transparent robe, wearing a black masquerade mask.

Alice was looking so seductive. From the top of the mask came curls of curly brown hair that brushed across her shoulders and touched the top of her boobs. I felt something romantic would emerge from this relationship because I trusted my sixth sense. When I looked at her, I noticed her nipples were erect, and her breast was perky round. I signalled her to lie down on the couch like Rose, and she stepped gradually and opened the dress in front of me. Because we were both women, Alice was far more comfortable standing naked in front of me. Alice came out of the sheer dress, entirely naked; I admired her warm, ebony body, from her complete and firm breasts to her curved hips and shaved crotch. I could see her clit emerging from her pussy. My eyes investigated every detail of her gorgeous body. As I watched her nakedness, I felt my throat dry with excitement. The magnificent tattoo of 'Red Rose' was the pleasant attraction on her curved thighs. I felt warm and damp. How was it possible that the very fact of seeing Alice naked could make my body react that way?

While looking at her, I started feeling something for her, she came and posed on the couch like Rose, and without a word, I started sketching her. I tried to focus on my art, but her gleaming eyes on me distracted my focus from my work. While marking her beautiful body, I gave shape while rubbing her round breast with my fingers on the canvas; it made me feel like I was touching her smooth, shiny skin. Every part of her body encouraged me to manage it. I began to love her curly hair and the shape of her long, smooth legs. Alice also pleased me during my work, as if she was fully aware of my feelings for her. Alice once pulled her legs apart. When I saw her legs spread, my breath got heavier. Next, I saw Alice pushing her hand between her thighs and pushing one finger from her pussy. When Alice took her finger out of her pussy, it was shining with her pussy cream, a clear indication to me that she was horny. She brought her finger to her mouth and licked it as if it was the most delightful thing she'd ever tasted. Somehow, I was able to complete my sketch and show it.

The joy in her eyes was visible; she hugged me and kissed me on my lips, and I, too, kissed her in return. I started kissing her all over her body. Alice took my clothes off while I was kissing her. Her gentle hands touched my body. Her tongue darted between my lips, smooth and soft; her breath warmed me up as our breasts pushed against each other, as our breathing became more intense and more rapid. Alice was getting close to an inch; her beautiful boobs were right in front of me, and her dark eyes hit me. I swallowed a lot and wondered how I would feel if I had her nipples in my mouth. How will it feel to suck them? God, they would probably taste better than the best chocolate. Her curved breast was so inviting that I could not stop sucking her round, juicy breasts. We got horny and hungry for one another. She was wet just as I was.

I was as hot as the sun, which awakened my desire even more. I rode up to the bed, mounted on her face and lowered my pussy into her mouth. Her lips merged on my pussy lips, and she started eating my pussy. I leaned forward and shoved my tongue into her vaginal cavity. I licked her intimate area, and she licked mine. We rubbed our intimacy with pleasure and kissed each other. Our tongues were swirling round and round inside each other's pussy. Whenever Alice and my folds awoke, more intense, we took pleasure in all 69 positions. I painted her beautiful body with vibrant colours; I massaged every inch of her body with my hands. Alice got drowned in various nuances of colours. She looked no less than any masterpiece to me. Finally, the moment arrived when we both reached a high point. We both felt tired and lay completely naked on the clean, crispy white bed. We were in love;   I had realized my sexuality through Alice, and I am grateful to her because I discovered a lesbian inside my body at that moment.

After our first sex relationship, our life changed entirely, especially mine. We both were in love, and we were always in search of any slight chance to touch each other throughout the day. Sometimes by handling documents in the classroom or intentionally passing remarkably close to feel the touch. Our hide-and-seek games were always on in class. We always had fun with each other, sometimes in her bathroom, taking a shower together or sometimes in the corner of the silent library. As the days passed, our feelings remained constant.

One evening, I gave Alice a box. Since it was a Teachers' Day party, Alice and I had planned to have dinner at one of her favourite restaurants.

When Alice opened the package with enthusiasm, her eyes broadened with surprise when she found a long, thin object; she said, "Oh my God, it's a vibrator, it's a vibrator!"

So I inserted the battery, gave it to her, and told her to wear it at night before leaving for dinner.

"What's your plan, darling?" She asked me with love.

"Nothing, sweetie, I just want to please you", I answered her and left.

At night, as I waited for Alice at the restaurant, my throat dried up when I saw her enter the room. She wore a black dress that kissed her body sexually; her curved body was pointed out, and her tight ass was inviting. The dress was low-cut in the form of a V, and her neckline was very well-seen. The outfit was completed with heels, which made her look like a model.

"Jesus, Christ!" you are looking so damn hot. I hugged her as she walked in.

When we sat in our comfy chairs, I asked Alice, "Have you inserted the vibrator in your pussy".

Alice snickered and said, 'Yes.'

"So, how does it feel? ', I asked her.

"Weird," she added, "but I look forward to seeing what it is."

I smiled, and from my pocket, I removed a small black remote control and showed it from afar.

Then I asked Alice, "Are you ready for the pleasure, my sexy woman".

As I was about to press the button waiter came toward us, and we both got busy deciding on our menu. Eventually, we ordered wine and cream lobster. When our wines arrived midway through our drink, Alice jumped when she felt the vibrator come to life in her pussy, vibrating on her tender pussy walls.

Helen, what are you up to? Don't you realize we're in a public place," Alice asked as she wiped her lips with a towel?

She was all fired up simultaneously but trying to look normal.

"It's a pleasure, my dear, to turn you on while we're here," I said and pressed the other button on the remote.

The vibrator in Alice was tracking down her G-spot. Alice appeared terribly hot and intense. It was hard for her to finish her drink.

"Let's go to the ladies' room, my dear, for a few minutes so we can refresh ourselves, if you know what I mean, Helen," said Alice.

So she asked the waiter, "Where is the washroom, please?"

Over there, the waiter pointed towards it.

Alice was shaking with desire as we both went to the bathroom. We found an empty booth, and we both went inside. Alice was quick to close the door. While the vibrator was penetrating her vagina, I pulled Alice into my arms and kissed her with longing and lust. I massaged Alice's tits through the soft material. Alice's nipples were horny, and with my fingers, I was touching her boobs and giving her the pleasure of feeling sexy. Alice was in a state of an explosion, sensing that she would explore with longing and delight.

The two of us were in a public place and controlling our moans. I put my hands on Alice's vibrator and gently pushed the vibrator deeper into her cunt. Alice lost herself in heaven and groaned gently. Alice felt a pleasure so intense that she had to bite to avoid moaning loudly. We had sex many times at different times and places, but that experience was at a higher level. We have never experienced so much pleasure.

Outside the cabin, we had tension when we heard the bathroom door open and female voices, but Alice didn't seem to care. Instead, she embraced me, moving the vibrator inside and outside with one hand. Each instant was hard and fast, bringing it closer to its peak. Finally, Alice's breath became heavy because she knew she was near the most tremendous orgasm of her life.

"Oh fuck, you are almost there," I moaned softly in her mouth.

"Harder, Helen, Harder," she said, shaking my hand and pushing the vibrator inside and outside.

At that point, Alice didn't care if somebody in the bathroom listening to her. Her pussy crushed with her orgasm, and she sensed the juice oozing.

"Happy Teacher's Day," I said and licked her cream.

Every day flowed through deep love and a strong connection between us. Alice was in love with me and was the only person I was crazy about.

It was the first Valentine's Day. We were both in despair for that day in our lives; after spending ten months together, valentine's evening was extremely special to us. All day, we both were prepping for the night. I was extremely mindful of Alice's choices because I knew she loved luxurious perfumes. But being a student, I wasn't in a position where I could afford such an expensive gift. As a result, I borrowed money from my parents and close friends for a memorable evening.

I invited her to one of those high-priced bars away from home. I was desperate to meet her across the street.

Time was running so slowly while waiting for her. As my eyes were on a constant search for her face on the street, I encountered Alice waving at me from the other side of the road and imitating me to stay.

Alice looked so pretty in the red floral dress that I couldn't let her out of my sight. She was coming to meet me with many red roses in her hand with a bright smile on her lips. We were both lost in each other eyes while I was desperately waiting to take her in my arms. It was as though time had ceased, and there was no one between us and around us. Then, in a split second, there was a tremendous noise, and I was in shock. The beautiful moment had turned into a fearful sight. I could not scream, lost my voice, and saw a colossal agitation. The police siren and the paramedics' alarm kept ringing in my ears. I've been looking everywhere for Alice. The last image of her in my memory was that she was coming toward me with red roses and a shining smile.

In the commotion, when I returned to my sense, I recalled waiting for her on the other side of the road when the group of drunken youths impatiently hit her severely in a split second. I went after Alice, and I found her lying on the street. When I ran toward her, Alice's beautiful face was entirely in the blood. I grabbed Alice in my arms and started to scream. I was crying uncontrollably. I was dealing with a panic crisis at that time. There was immediate help from an ambulance, but she was declared dead in the hospital.

There are times when circumstances change; nothing is permanent in life; I learned this after Alice passed away.

It has been ten years, and I still visit Alice's grave without fail. After Alice left, I quit medical science and picked my passion. Yet, I still have the sketch of my Rose, where I met the love of a lifetime. Alice was the natural 'She' who had turned me on and showed me an authentic side of Her inside me.

Dark Secret

My name is Nitin Chopra. Five years ago, I worked as a paramedic in a hospital in Russia. I was single and wanted to settle down with one of my lovely sweetheart Priya, who was studying medicine in India. My family was aware of my feelings for her, except for Priya herself. So, I always tried to come closer to her, but she always tried not to respond as I expected. And that quality of hers got me more in love with her. It was not that she was not in love with me, she was in love with me, but somehow, she was reluctant to approach. Priya was a sweet, gentle girl with attractive features.

We were in love, and she never spent a day without speaking to me. I used to write a few poems for her, and while reading, she used to blush. Her shyness was the best thing that kept bringing me down for her repeatedly. Finally, one day, with all my courage, I proposed to her, and she said, 'Yes' without hesitation. Her 'yes' was the incredible commitment that she had given to me. I was on a new cloud after listening to her yes, and I had a lot of sleepless nights imagining Priya as my wife. One night we both kissed; it was the first time we had tasted one another. Her kiss was sweeter than the maple syrup.

After a long wait, that precious day eventually came into our lives, and we tied the knot forever. Before tying the knot, Priya had only one request she didn't want to leave India and settle in Russia. As she didn't want to leave her parents behind so far. I fell in love with her more because of her decision; I accepted her request and left Russia. So I moved to India and got a new job and home. We were so happy the day we were married; she looked so pretty in her pink dress. My eyes got stuck on her beauty, and I silently thanked God and my stars for giving me this joy. It was a grand wedding.

Our first night was beautiful; she looked so sexy in her blue satin gown. I wanted to touch and feel her. I tried to embrace her and treasure her forever. Our first night was not so horny as Priya was uncomfortable with me. She hesitated about opening her heart to me. It was natural, and I was not in any rush to throw myself at her. I realized she needed time, and I should give her that space to feel comfortable about new things in her life.

We were friends, but now we are spouses, so some things have changed. As the days went by, we came closer together, and she became comfortable. Each day I admired her beauty, and simultaneously, I lost the patience to feel her. Finally, after three weeks, I dared to have an intimate relationship with Priya at midnight. She was still uncomfortable, but I decided I would never leave her that night; whatever happened, I would make love to her. I went to great lengths to make her feel that intimacy, and as a result, she began to enjoy pleasure. She accepted me with unconditional love without any hesitation. I licked her round breast and gave her a hard blow on the bed, and she was moaning with ecstasy. I did not miss a single expression on her face; it seemed more beautiful to me.

Each night was a night of love, the enchanting beauty of Priya completely drowned me, but one thing was always there: Priya never took her first step to come toward me. One evening, I came home early and found her away. I called her to verify, and she said she was with her friend. That night, Priya showed up extremely late and looked exhausted. I asked her if everything were okay; she responded with a flippant yes and said she was tired and would like to rest. So, being a good husband, I, too, slept that night with her without being intimate.

The following day at the breakfast table, I was planning our honeymoon with Priya. I thought hearing about the honeymoon plan would make her dance happily. But I was surprised that she had no interest in her honeymoon. That was shocking to me. I wondered why Priya did not care about the honeymoon. Come on, every married woman awaits such beautiful moments in her life, and when that moment is knocking at her door, she refuses to answer them. I love her, and she loves me then; what was the matter? I thought I could convince her to go on our honeymoon soon.

One day, I was searching for some papers in my drawer when I came across some erotic accessories like a vibrator, handcuff, and sexy lingerie. First, I laughed aloud because I had never seen such things personally and thought seeing these accessories on my shelf was hilarious. Second, I was surprised to see Priya planning a sexy dance with me, I thought. So, I quietly kept those things on the square as appropriate as earlier because my intentions were not to ruin Priya's surprise.

I was desperately looking forward to the night. Eventually, I went to bed when it got dark and started fantasizing about Priya in that lingerie. In my fantasies, she looked stunning diva in her red lace lingerie as she came toward me with those black leather handcuffs. She took my hands, gently embraced me, and then tied my hands to the corner of the bed. While attaching my hands, her round breast touched my lips, and I licked her nipples. Priya sat on top of me and took off her dress little by little, piece by piece. I felt her bare skin, and she showed me her hot moves. Her soft, bare skin was glowing, and her cups were hanging from top to bottom as she took advantage of the sexy ride on me. All those fantasies turned me on, and I felt my manliness harden. I waited for Priya to come as quickly as possible, as it had become difficult to control. When I heard Priya come in, I immediately turned off the light and pretended to sleep, making it more comfortable for her to start the show. Priya got into bed, but I did not touch her; there was a secret smile on my lips, my eyes were closed, and I was waiting desperately for her first move. After five minutes, I could not feel anything from her side. I wondered what was wrong. So, I turned to look; to my surprise, I saw she was busy tapping on the phone with a smile on her lips. I asked her whom she was communicating with at that late hour, and she answered, "Friend."

"You close your eyes," she said.

I turned my back on her one more time. I stared at the wall clock. Ten minutes later, I turned my head to watch her from the corner of my eye. Her eyes were constantly fixed on the screen. I missed her body by my side.

Finally, she looked at me and said, "Two minutes . . . is all . . . I need to say good night to my friend."

A friend? Nonsense!! Who is that friend? Come on; there should be a name for this friend. That sort of frustration flowed through my mind. I was not a conservative sort of husband. I do not mind if my wife has a male friend, but she should involve me in her life. She should introduce me to every one of her friends. At that moment, my mind was grappling with all kinds of questions. And then a seed of doubt broke out in my mind: Does my wife have an affair with somebody? Does my wife have another man in her life? I was just losing my mind and my patience. Finally, I decided to comprehend and catch Priya red-handed.

The next day, I told Priya that I would be home late, so there was no need to wait for me for dinner. Priya nodded and grinned. I was more shocked by this kind of cold reaction from my wife.

How can a wife not even express herself? Won't she even miss me? Or is she a very understanding wife? Has she come with a no-problem manual? Does she deeply understand her husband's work of nature? Rather than question her, I should be proud of her sense of compassion. I sipped my coffee and left the house in a confused state of mind.

After I left my house, I parked my car a long way under the huge banyan tree to see the door of my house. I decided to monitor Priya's activities. Who comes into my house or with whom does she encounters every little thing in my absence? I spent two hours in my car, and there was no activity. I called Priya to track her down. Priya casually replied and said she would spend her day at home.

After finishing my appeal, I changed my mind and was embarrassed to doubt my wife. I shook my head and was about to go around the corner when I saw the main door of my house open. I saw Priya emerge from the house. She was waiting outside and talking to somebody over the phone. Priya was looking happy and beautiful as usual. When I saw her grinning and playing with her hair, I fell in love with her again. I was feeling sorry I doubted Priya. She was my wife; how did I suspect her; I was supposed to leave the place and stop thinking nonsense about Priya. But my spirit compelled me not to change my decision as her husband. I wanted to prove myself wrong in all ways. I love Priya, and she loves me; that is all I care about.

As I was heading out of the corner, I saw a red car parked near Priya. Someone of, a tall figure, came out of the vehicle, and they hugged each other. It was not a friendly cuddle; they were kissing each other. Watching Priya kissing, my eyes got wet, and I felt like my instinct was right for the first time in my life. I could not see that person very clearly; only I could see a long mantle and a hat. After meeting and greeting, Priya sat in his car and within seconds, they left. I took my car right away and began to follow them. They went to a cottage about thirty minutes away from my residence. I parked my car out of the way and saw them walking hand in hand. I was angry to see Priya's romantic side with someone. Seeing Priya with him, it was easy to understand that the relationship was not new; they had been in love before marriage. But if Priya was in love with him, what made her marry me? I would have never asked her to marry me if she had expressed her feelings honestly for someone. Why did she cheat on my innocent feelings? Why did she make a mess of everything? My heart cried out for Priya's explanation.

I got out of my car and started walking around the yard. There were thick giant trees, and I hid behind a large tree trunk because I did not want

Priya to see me. There were many windows, and it was difficult to encounter them in those similar windows. I looked around; a few people were outside the cottage, few children and families were also in the large swimming pool area. Many people occupied a stall around the restaurant. There was loud music around the pool. While my eyes were searching, I saw Priya entering one of the rooms. I got out of the back of the tree and started walking toward that room. I glanced at the room from the outside; a 'No Disturb' tag was hanging on the doorknob. I felt like banging or knocking on the door for a while, but it won't make me grab Priya and her lover red-handed. I started searching for ways to enter her room; while I was thinking, I saw a small lane going behind her room which could help me to enter inside from the balcony. Very calmly, I walked behind space.

The backyard was entirely surrounded by giant trees and utter silence. To reach the balcony, I needed ladders. Their room was on the ground floor, so it was not as difficult to enter the balcony. After looking here and there, I found two substantial rough rocks on the ground. I climbed on those stones, and with the support of a fence, I mounted the enclosure of the balcony connected to the living room. Once on the patio, I concealed myself behind the glass doors. Before entering, I cast a secret glance at the living room. It was vacant. There were just a couple of drinks on the table.

I opened the glass door and slowly walked into the drawing room. I discovered that there was another piece of glass sliding door connected, which was partially pulled down from the drapes. It was a bedroom.

Priya and her lover were in that room. I went by the room, and before I opened the door, I hid behind those curtains as I could see something. It wasn't that clear, but it was not hard for me to get the view inside. I must have seen only a few things like the bed corner, coffee table and wall clock. I saw Priya coming out of the bathroom, standing between the bed and me. Priya had worn that red lingerie I had found in the drawer; she was dancing in front of the bed. I saw Priya take off her lingerie across from that man. Only I could not catch a glimpse of that man because the bed was in such a position that the end part of the bed was visible to my view. But it was sure there was someone on the bed.

By that time, I had felt death's pain a million times. I wanted to commit suicide, believing that Priya, my beloved wife, was with someone. I was begging God to wake me up from my sleep and never show me those weird things again in my dream. But, the reality was dancing shamelessly in front of my eyes; my wife was involved with someone. Priya betrayed my love and trust and threw all my love away without caring about me. After ruining my world, how can she be so happy? She was jumping on the bed; it seemed like she was enjoying her burgeoning orgasm. Amid all this, I saw two hands holding Priya's round buttocks; it was clear that someone was enjoying her wild naked ride. That was when I lost all my patience and control over all my emotions. The entire sentiment converted my tears into a burning rage of anger and vengeance.

I quietly opened the sliding door a bit. I heard Priya moaning. From her moans, it was easy to figure out that she was with someone, and it can never be easy for a husband to see his wife enjoying sex with someone. I wanted to hurt Priya and that man. I was searching for something to beat them hard. When I was snooping around, I saw a knife on the table. I grabbed that knife and went straight to the bedroom.

As I walked into the room, I saw Priya lying on the bed, and that man was inside the duvet licking her pussy. Priya was in a very intimate mood; I had never seen her like this before. After witnessing her affair, all my love for Priya vanished like thin air. Seeing Priya with somebody on the bed, my character changed.

I became evil; with full force, I stabbed that man. Priya started screaming, and I stabbed him to death. I lost all my senses and just wanted to kill him for turning my life into a living hell. I do not know how many times I stabbed him in anger. Priya was continuously yelling like a maniac. As I turned my head toward Priya, she took her clothes from the chair, pushed me hard down, and ran for help. I wanted to stab Priya, too, but I was shocked when I pulled out the duvet. My shirt was entirely stained with blood. I became a psychopath; my senses stopped working while I was killing that person. Blood ran through the victim, and the white bed had turned completely red. I remained struck that the unknown lover was not a man. A woman's naked body was lying on the bed; she was my wife's lover. Priya was dating a woman. My wife was lesbian. In this commotion, I found the same vibrator in the bloody hands of the dead woman. All the pieces of puzzles started settling in my mind. After marriage, why did Priya not want to settle with me in Russia, her night chat, away from home, coming home tired, do not want to go for a honeymoon and all those sex toys in the drawer?

It was too much for me to oversee; my wife Priya, whom I had loved with pure heart, was a lesbian. Finally, I realized why she was not at ease with me on the bed. Why does she always make a fake orgasm with me all the time? Priya never wanted her secret to reveal and hide this dark secret from her family and the entire world. Finally, to keep her secret locked, she agreed to marry me.

When reality came before me, I became a maniac, weeping and laughing at the two moments. My mental health has broken down. And when I came to my senses, I ended up in a loony bin with crazy people around me. Out of that, I was arrested.

Now I am rotting in jail, and I do not want to live anymore in this world. That faint moment in my life turned me into a murderer. Priya divorced me, and I never told anybody about her dark secret. Within these four prison walls, I always ask myself these questions. What caused me so much anger? Seeing my wife sleep with somebody? Or the way she fooled me. I am still in search of that answer. I know my wife's gloomy secret. Whatever it was, one thing was true, my Priya, my wife, was a lesbian. Her dark secret had ruined my life forever and turned me into a murderer. Each day am rotting in this prison and waiting for my death to arrive.

Sweet sixteen

While smoking on the silent roof, I watched a video of my friend's daughter on social media. My friend was celebrating her daughter's sixteen birthday, 'SWEET SIXTEEN,' as mentioned in her caption. I smiled, and that same bag of guests came to my mind. *Why do teenagers always look forward to their 16th birthday? Is there something special?* All these questions were still inside my brain. Age has always been a number; what difference does it make if you are sixteen or seventeen? How come there are no words like Sweet Seventeen? Does this mean that when we are sixteen, we are sweet? After that, we taste bitter? Before I have the flashback, let me take one last whiff of my cigarette.

Yes, now let us go to the flashback of my story.

I (Nancy) was sixteen, not just a sweet sixteen-year-old, and Elaine is now my wife; we were both in the same high school in Texas. Although we were in the same school, we never spoke or met.

Something was amusing; we both had a mutual friend, Den. It was my 16th birthday party; this was the first time Elaine and I got introduced correctly by Den. At that party, I had the hots for her, but the saddest part was she was straight. She was at a party with her boyfriend, so I overcame the urge. I remember seeing her kissing and dancing with her boyfriend at that party, and I felt terrible to see both happy together. As a teenager, I drank a lot at that party. I wondered if my fortune played a stupid kind of prank on me. The first time my age turned sixteen, seeing Elaine with her boyfriend turned my particular age from sweet into sour. It made me feel like somebody sprinkled lots of chillies and pepper at the age of sweetness—my heart got gripped by pain and sadness.

Until I met Elaine, I was not an enthusiastic fan of swimming lessons, but I never missed swimming lessons after I was with Elaine. Even though we were waving and meeting at school, Elaine still treated me like an ordinary friend without knowing my feelings for her. During swimming lessons, she had changed in front of me several times; we even took showers together. In the shower, I rubbed her back, and Elaine petted mine. But I always retained control because I had always been clear in my mind that she had a boyfriend. So, all I cared about was hanging out with her.

Elaine was a class senior, and the day came when she graduated. After graduation, my happy days vanished because she produced good news that she would pursue her career in acting. Finally, one day came in my life when I said bye to her at the airport as Elaine was going to start a new chapter in her life in an acting academy in NYC. Watching her go, I thought I would never spend time with her again because now she would have more new friends and soon forget about our friendship. As I was sure about her that she was immensely talented and beautiful. One day I would see her winning awards on television and read her interview in various magazines. I was completely confident that she would turn into a huge celebrity.

It was summer days after my graduation. Elaine came back. I was shocked when I found out she did not want to be an actress. Elaine left her theatre school and wanted to do something different, regular work in New York. I want to confess that when I saw her back, I was thrilled, and I was more pleased to know that she had also changed her mind about becoming an actress. As she had left her a year earlier, somehow, Elaine did not seem so cheerful anymore. I tried to ask her several times, but she still claimed everything was normal. As a friend, I never wanted to force her to tell the truth because I thought she would be better off on time. Also, we both come from a small town, and being a lesbian is something Elaine would never consider me. Something was wrong with Elaine, I was sure.

One day, I found her weeping when I went to her place. Seeing her devastated, I crossed every line of friendship and forced her to tell me about the reasons for her sadness. That was when I learned that Elaine's boyfriend cheated on her. Her boyfriend was dating her friend from the acting class. Not because she was talented or beautiful. It was because she was rich. Her fancy lifestyle attracted Elaine's boyfriend. The most awful and hurtful behaviour was that he did not even bother to look for Elaine after the breakup or try to come back. When Elaine returned to Texas, he never even visited her. Finally, Elaine discovered he was getting engaged to the same girl. And as a result, Elaine was broken. She did not want to tell me all that because she thought she could get through it. I tried to hold her in my arms and make her feel secure, but I controlled my feelings about touching her. After hearing that, I told Elaine to forget everything that had happened in the past. There was no reason to regret anything now.

Somehow, I made her understand and tried to calm her mood down. At that time, Elaine's loneliness was my priority; I started caring for Elaine and always made sure to spend more time with her. Little by little, the two of us began spending time together, sometimes going to the park in the evening, eating, shopping, watching movies or reading books silently.

After spending all that time together, Elaine realized her feelings for me. Besides hiding my feelings, I never wanted to reveal my truth. Sometimes it is hard to explain, and one can lose one's friendship. I was afraid I might lose her if I told my truth. So, seeing her happy, I was delighted. And mentally, I was making myself more vital to that day when Elaine would be satisfied with somebody else. I had always heard and read that the opposite poles attracted, but that did not work for me. She was not a lesbian, so it was not her fault, I was a lesbian, so it was not my fault, either.

One summer, we were both hanging out. We were swimming on the beach when Elaine fell in love with me. In her eyes, there was love for me, but I pretended not to notice it. Till she says nothing, I cannot be sure. The issues of lesbianism are sensitive. So I didn't mean to do or say anything wrong that would affect Elaine's feelings. That night, we watched a movie and were awake until 3:00 a.m., talking about nothing and everything. And coincidentally, we were watching movies about lesbians.

Finally, Elaine bravely asked me, "How would you feel if I said I would love to kiss you on your sexy lips, Nancy?"

I was shocked and surprised at the same time to hear those words coming from Elaine's mouth. I had to look at her face to see if she was serious and not making fun of me. She looked at me seriously to get my response. My heart was jammed in my throat at the thought that I could read her movements on me wrong and Elaine could say no and reject me.

Elaine's beautiful eyes were on me; she drank wine and said, "Think about it," I insisted.

Elaine got up, opened up the lace on her dress, and said, "I always thought the relationships between women were pretty interesting, and sometimes I was tempted to try it."

I was excited by the thought, and I felt my pussy begin to crawl with excitement.

Elaine instantly caught my facial expression and asked, "Are you blushing?"

"No, but it never occurred to me," I lied.

My words and eyes were not coordinated with one another at that moment. I saw Elaine smile as if she had understood my falsehood. She slowly took steps toward me; as she approached me and stood, I began to appreciate the sexual tension that was mounting among us. Elaine came to me, pulled the clamps out of my hair, and untied my hair with her soft, feathery hands.

At that point, it became hard for me to control my feelings for her which I had held for a long time. I kissed her pretty hard. And within a second, Elaine grabbed me and kissed me fervently. Elaine and I went upstairs to the bedroom, and Elaine began to undress immediately, without any concern for who was watching.

Elaine's kiss was full of rapture and feeling. Our tongues swirled one with the other. She unzipped my dress, untied my bra, and took my breast mounds in her hands. We were nude together, and our bodies touched smoothly and gently. I started massaging her breasts, taking Elaine's big, hard tits between my fingers and wrapping them in half-circles. My body was alive to the fullest. Elaine was sensing the dampness between my legs. I was able to see Elaine; she was having fun with me. Elaine enveloped her lips around my nipple and began to suck it; it hardened like her hard nipples. We both sensed the heat of our skin. I dropped kisses all over her neck and collarbone while she was crushing my hips. She looked so beautiful when she enjoyed the pleasure of my fingers within herself; she resembled a goddess of sex. Her breast and nipples gave me the joy of loving her even more.

Then, we started making out, and I said to her, "I've never gone down on a girl, and I really want to. Do you want to try it?"

She was similarly interested. I was so excited! I had no idea what I was doing, so I let my instincts get in. Elaine spread her legs to give me more access to her sex. I slipped my finger into her drenched pussy. I grabbed a finger while pulling, leaving it near the most sensitive point of Elaine's pussy, her G-spot, and Elaine let out a big moan.

"Of course, Elaine." I've dreamed of these moments for so long," I murmured.

We started to satisfy each other with our mouths and even inserted fingers in each other's cunt and licked the clit. Ultimately, we both reached a climax and swallowed each other's love juices.

The experience was so natural and liberating. It was also rare to feel overpowered and in control with a sexual partner. That night had turned into such a beautiful one between us. We both loved each other a lot without any hesitations.

When the first sun rays entered our room, I opened my eyes and found Elaine asleep beside me. It was a fantastic morning for me. I had never fallen in love with the morning earlier in my life, but spending the night with Elaine made my morning extraordinary. Elaine clasped me in her arms when I saw her beauty. I wanted to kiss her again on her soft pink lips, but then I felt Elaine would regret what happened between us after coming back to her senses. I don't want Elaine's morning to get a little awkward. Tears flowed across my cheeks as the thought of my beautiful friendship ended. Before she had any regrets, I silently wore my clothes and prepared to open the door button. Elaine's soft hands held my hand as I was about to open the door knob. She looked gorgeous in her long brown hair, and her lips invited me to kiss her again. Our friendship had turned so strong that we could read each other's minds without saying anything. Elaine told me that what happened in the night was her decision, and there was nothing to be doubtful about. She loves me, gladly enjoys being with me forever, and has no interest in any man despite her heterosexuality. I sensed it would be an injustice to Elaine, so I confessed to her about myself. I have said everything about myself and how I feel since I saw her at Den's party. I also told her that she did not have to be with me because we both got intimate. She has a life out there, and there must be someone to carry her through. There can be no match between a lesbian and a heterosexual girl. But Elaine denied it all; she kissed me again and told me that she had already given me her heart, and now there was no way to go to anyone. If she is not with me, she will not be with anyone.

And after listening to Elaine, I surrendered my decisions and thoughts. I never thought Elaine would have feelings for me. Being a lesbian myself, it was my practice to have feelings for the other girl. But Elaine was no lesbian, and she had feelings, which was a miracle for me. So, my prayers have been fulfilled. Now Elaine and me we have been together ever for sixteen years together. Yes, our sweet sixteen years, we cherish the sweetness of being together each day. Sometimes, when I see Elaine with me, I realize that there are no lesbians, men, or women in society. All that brings two people together is pure love and mutual understanding. There is no correspondence between lesbian and heterosexual we are both like two different poles, but now I sense yes, sometimes, opposite poles react with each other.

My thoughts were interrupted when I heard a sweet voice, "Nancy!"

"Yes"

"Will you stop counting the stars on the rooftop now? Come to bed too late now," Elaine stands with her arms crossed and waits for Nancy to come in.

"Yes, babe, let us go . . . I love you."

Elaine kisses Nancy while kissing Nancy; Elaine gently whispers, "I love you too. Happy sixteenth anniversary to both of us."

The Sex Toy

What gets into you when you hear the word 'SEX'?

'Sex' by hearing that word makes us tickle in our sensitive zone, brings a naughty smile to our lips and a bit of excitement in our monotonous life for a while. Honestly, we all desire sex secretly or boldly. We all want a great sex life, but some still fear 'sex'. They cannot even imagine being told that word in their lives. I am in this category not because I am spiritual or an exceptionally good girl but because I know I will have no man with whom I can enjoy my sexual life. Men need beautiful women, and many have secretive desires to get intimate with women. They want the woman to have a beautiful look, a sexy body, and the art of lovemaking. I have nothing against men who believe in equal opportunities. When we women demand a good-looking prince charming, then why not men? But what about those personalities that aren't adorable, either with sexy bodies or shapes that women should go in? Is there a handsome, attractive man who falls in love with an uninformed and unattractive woman and is prepared to make her his life partner? If any of you know this kind of man, take control of this planet without wasting any second, and please let me know.

By the time I finished grade tenth, I was overly excited about studying in the upper class. I always pictured myself with a man who would love me for who I am, not for my beauty. When I began high school, I was obsessed with a handsome guy from my class. I had always fantasized about him on the bed with me in various positions. My preferred place was as a cowgirl. Secretly I was fond of reading Kamasutra books and always curious to know more about sex. But being a girl, I was taught to stand behind the curtains of shyness. So, I spent my days admiring this guy, but one day my obsessions turned into tears. He was making out with some other girl in the library. That night I finished my two packets of tissue boxes. So, my first story, which did not even begin, ended.

After a few days, I emerged from this love fever and focused on my studies, but that did not last long until our principal arrived with a beautiful personality. Our principal introduced the new music teacher to the class. He was a young, mature, handsome man. He wasn't like any other boring teacher. I began to enjoy the music class and was always enthusiastic to hear his musical voice. Whatever melody he played, I would smell it for myself. However, seeing his smooth fingers on the piano while playing always wounded my heart with the Cupid arrows.

It was Valentine's Day, and we had a Valentine's Day celebration at our high school. I decided to confess my feelings and tell him on this special day? To make my Valentine more special, I took a heart-shaped balloon and knelt before him; suddenly, I asked him to be my Valentine.

I went and expressed my attraction towards him, but he only smiled and said, "This is your infatuation, dear. Very soon, you will be out of this phase. This happens to everyone, but at present, you should only focus on your studies."

Upon hearing his reply, I busted several red balloons that dark night. And my other story too soon got ended.

Life was going on without any passion. All my friends were seeing someone and spending more quality time with their loved ones. Slowly, my handful of friends began to disappear from my life. My life just got very dull. And in this monotonous life, I found myself a new boyfriend.

'Obesity' was a new boy friend of mine every time I saw other happy girls with someone, it always depressed me. And in that depressed state, I started eating junk food and went lazy. There was no difference between Garfield and me. Days passed by, lying on the couch and switching channels. Not a single TV show, news, songs, or movie could make me happy.

But then it all changed one morning when I saw a new handsome, charming face in front of the window. The man was doing push-ups on his balcony. I immediately grabbed my phone and took his picture. "What the . . ." I didn't move until that guy disappeared into his room next door.

"What the fuck. . .," Upon seeing him, I said: "This hot guy is my new Neighbour; how come I did not even notice him until now?"

He was filled with Tom Cruise features. We all heard the girl next door, but there was a seductive man next door in my story. Somewhere, my depressive counter was going down, and my level of obsession was rising up . . . one more time.

I began stalking him on social networks. From my window, I discovered that he was single and on his own. I do not know why I was so obsessed with him, but I became fond of him. And I wanted him to love me back.

One night, I was driving home from the supermarket. I met my new Neighbour next to my doorstep. He looked so handsome and hot in those sports outfits. As we opened our doors, he smiled at me and greeted me. I, too, smiled back and greeted him. He kindly introduced himself to me and asked me to come for coffee. At that moment, I was flying in the air; I immediately threw my groceries bags on my sofa and went into his house. He was not only handsome but also an extremely systematic person. Of course, being alone in the house, all his things were still in the right place and appropriate. No mess, no shabby clothes here and there, and everything were clean.

He was quick to get two hot mugs of coffee, and in a short time, we both talked about diverse topics on film and television shows, and the exciting thing was he was an RJ in the music studio. So, within thirty minutes, we started making connections. I was under the impression that he loved me, too. I always wanted to make out with him and feel him all over my body. So, whenever he would talk to me, in my head, I would make out and sleep with him in distinct positions. I have no idea how often I have crushed the bed with him in my dreams.

One night, we sat on our rooftops admiring the stars. I spoke about my feelings for him.

He looked at me seriously, and after a minute break, he started laughing aloud and told me, "I don't want to sound rude to you, but I am sorry, dear. Have you seen yourself? I mean, see your size; you are like a football. Come on, think practical. I can never picture myself with you as I already have many beautiful girlfriends in my life. Am I crazy to walk away from them and be with you"?

His words wounded my heart; all he wanted was to be my friend and nothing more. So, my Neighbour's story . . . also ended . . . right then.

I got rejected three times because of the way I looked. Enough was enough. I began to dislike men. After my three denials, one thing was clear: they deserve no love; they never know what love is. All they need is a beautiful body, a charming face and nothing. I decided that now I would hunt down no man in my life and live my life according to my terms. Just because I am not beautiful, I will not give the right to anyone to break my heart. To express love for them made me feel like begging for love.

After my third and last heartbreak, something changed inside me. Things started to turn around in my life, and I started making friends only with girls and women. Sometimes, I crave men's affection and love, but at that point, all those unpleasant memories would torture me; as a result, I would immediately separate myself from those wild cravings. My love for girls has made me better and happier, the way love should. I do not remember loving a guy who ever did me any good, and my whole previous love for men feels like a ghost.

****

Two Years Later . . .

I had matured a lot, and my body opened up as a real woman. I had my sexual impulses, of course, but every time these feelings came to life, I used to screw with my fingers to relieve myself, which worked for me.

I put more lip gloss on my lips and added mascara. I dressed in a short, tight dress that showed my sexy silhouette, gigantic ass, and luscious thighs. I clipped my hair and walked out.

I enjoyed a few glasses with my friends when one of my friends mentioned her experience using a vibrator. When I listened to her, a sort of curiosity sprang up in me. And right at that dinner table, I decided I would love to try this toy.

The following night, I was surfing the Internet when my eyes popped up on something fascinating. I saw Vibrator. A new challenge has sprung up in me while looking at the shape of many colourful vibrators to satisfy my hunger for intimacy. But this time, it was about no one; it was about me. So, I ordered a pricey vibrator for myself right away. And within 24 hours, I received my order.

In the night I opened my parcel and found a long vibrator.

This is going to be interesting, I thought. I got a new toy, my *'Sex Toy.'*

Seeing the Vibrator, I felt compelled to feel this wonderful thing more forcefully. An adjustable ring with a cushion provided pleasure: the more influential the bullet, the more intense the sensations it offers. The Vibrator is shaped like a male penis. There was a great feeling of touching and feeling this Vibrator. I took a long sip of wine before putting the glass on my nightstand. I let the soft liquid slowly slide down my throat before lying on the bed and letting out a long breath. My time finally came. With the flavour of red wine on my lips, I gently let my hands glide over my body. I carefully placed my fingers on the tip of the Vibrator while I was lying on my bed, holding the Vibrator with both hands.

My throat dried up in excitement, and my heartbeat increased to feel it in me. I kissed it and opened my mouth to suck the vibrator. It gave me the feeling as am being intimate with a man. The supple rubber vibrator made me more excited and insane. I noticed the hard points of my breasts pushing against the fabric of my cat and ran my fingertips around in circles. I arched my back like little tingles of pleasure energized my body. To experience this Vibrator, I made sure not to wear any fabric on my body. I undressed, slid the Vibrator out of my mouth to my neck, and then moved the Vibrator around my thick, round breast. The touch of the Vibrator excited my nipple, and I felt the sensation of moisture between my two curvy thighs. While moving the Vibrator down, I felt incredibly nervous, afraid of what and how? I wanted to experience it, but at some point, I was worried. I stuck my feet on the bed and spread my knees as both hands massaged my internal thighs.

I closed my eyes and imagined all those handsome faces of my past with whom I craved pleasure. I felt my fear, anxiety, and stress level fade away. There were eight different vibration modes, from 'pulse to 'cha-cha' to 'wave'. Slowly, I slipped the Vibrator and embedded it in me. And then there was a 'boom!!.

I shuddered as the vibrations penetrated deep into my core. I popped off in a millisecond. I could feel the man's dick in my clitoris. The vibrator movement made me feel like such a playful person. Tremors and training have brought me out of my ecstasy without shame. I could listen to my groaning with the full sound of intimacy. The Vibrator has given me all kinds of familiarity, pleasure and drives that a man can never give me. I was enjoying myself on my cosy bed. Finally, when I reached my climax, I took the Vibrator out softly inside me and felt like I had a beautiful ride of sex. I was amazed at myself because I never thought I had so much energy. I started feeling each part of my body so beautiful and sexy. So many men may fail with me upon the bed; I have so much love and passion for giving. *Why do men enjoy sleeping with women?* I thought. Just because they want it or their stress hormones to flow free. Men only fuck women because they want to remove all their stress hormones and feel good, but do they even know why women love to fuck men? Because she loves them with absolute passion and desire. Therefore, even after being fucked, she ardently wants her man to touch her, hear her love talk and love her all night.

After finishing the vibrator session, I cleaned it thoroughly and kept it near my bed drawer because I found my man. I started crying hard; my tears were irresistible because those bad memories shone in my brain when three good-looking men rejected me. I was not beautiful. No men were interested in peeping inside my heart. Most men are fond of stunning looks; they do not have the sense to understand women's hearts. That night, I wept a great deal of happiness and sorrow. That was the last night in my life when I thought about all those stupid losers.

I have the feeling that being a lesbian is the only choice for me. I concluded that my past attraction to men has only brought me unhappiness, tears, and rejections, but now I think: what is the point? So, what if I genuinely liked men back then? I am satisfied with my sex toy because this toy meets my desires without any conditions or humiliation. It does not alter that I only want to love women now, which is inside me, and that is all that matters.

I, Me & Myself

We have two genres in this world. All genders have two different body parts, which is the key to attracting opposite genders. And under the law of nature, men are supposed to like women and vice versa. And because of that process, children are born. And in the everyday world, it works. Such ordinary activity seems appropriate for the regular type of person. But what about a unique personality like mine? Where am I supposed to go?

Before I proceed, I would like to introduce myself to you.

My name is Sapna Roy. I am in my thirties and have been very frustrated since birth. Being born into an Indian conservative family, I have been an inconsistent force to compromise with my choices. Since childhood, I have loved boys' toys, clothes, accessories, and hairstyles. But having a girl's body, I was just meant to play with dolls instead of cars and guns. Wear colourful dresses rather than shirts and shorts, and always my hair length should continue to increase and tied in two ponytails. Only one thing was in my favour: I was only allowed to play with girls, and studying at a girls' school was overly exciting. But that excitement lasted for ten years; when I went to university, I saw girls and boys in bouquets hanging in every corner of the wall. Of course, there was nothing discriminatory between girls and boys. But as I was more comfortable with the girls around me since childhood, suddenly, seeing boys gave me a hesitant vibe. Somewhere I was constantly lacking in trust to see various boys here and there.

I had a friend named Rohan in my class. Only he was the guy I was comfortable with because he was friendly and helpful. From day one, he supported me and tried to take care of all my problems. He was a warm, caring person. He was the first guy in my classroom with whom I felt comfortable asking for his support during my assessments. At times, he also helped me in my studies. I never saw Rohan hanging around with other girls, and I didn't even bother to ask him why? We used to be good friends in class, but my attraction toward girls never decreased.

One day, our university board announced that all students would go on a field trip to Lonavala; all attendees were mandatory. It was a short drive from Mumbai. Being from a conservative family, my parents first did not allow me to be part of the trip. However, after explaining that the girls were also participating in the tour, their insecurity finally became convinced. My parents' mindset was that I would date some guy and have an affair, and with that affair, I would get pregnant, and the guy would refuse to marry me. As a result, I can commit suicide. For such kinds of thoughts, I certainly do not blame my parents. Because when my parents were kids, they would watch classic Bollywood movies every Friday, which showed the unwanted pregnancy of the actress. So, all thanks go to those kinds of crap movies. They thought it was happening everywhere and might also happen to their daughter. But they did not know their daughter's secret, that their daughter is only interested in girls, not boys. A lot of times, I wanted to explore and explain to them specifically about myself. Explain to them what I am? and what I am looking for in my life. But I know they can never understand me, so I do not blame them. They have never even heard a 'lesbian' word in their lives, and if they hear it, they will ask ten people around them to know what it means.

I was ready for the night off. Finally, before I took my bag, I touched my parents' feet to take their blessings. My parents were in tears, which was highly expected. They seemed anxious, and it was easy to understand that my trip was their number one concern. My mother held me in her arms and started with the chapter on the dignity of girls. She explained how daughters are the treasure of their parents, and I should always be careful for myself by not falling in love with someone and never bringing down my family name. I shook my head because the dialogue came from a full-length classic movie.

I grabbed my backpack and ran because I was choking on the weight of the girl's dignity.

As soon as I sat inside the cab, I rolled the glass out the window for fresh air. Cool air touched my face and made me want to feel myself. I wondered if I was a son, even though my parents might be more worried? Like, how they are now for me. When a daughter is born into a family, she brings a list of compromises and sacrifices she will make at every stage of her life. As I drowned in all these little thoughts, my cab stopped at the door of my college. All my classmates were waiting to get on the bus with their bags. I paid the fare, got out of the cab, and started walking in front. I heard my name from behind; the caller did not surprise me; it was Rohan. He immediately took my bag without my permission and told me to relax. At times I was afraid of Rohan's too-friendly attitude. I never understood why he was always forward in showing his attention and concern for me.

The two of us took the bus and took our seats. Rohan sat by my side, which made me a bit uncomfortable at first. I was expecting some girl near my seat. But, perhaps, I did not want to sound rude, so I did not mention anything to Rohan. As our journey started, we all had a lot of fun on the bus; we sang songs, cracked jokes, and over-ate chips. All the boys and girls were excited about this field trip, not because they were the type of hard-core students but just because they all were looking for fun and excitement in their adventurous life. And I was looking for a short break from my family's rules.

We had a short and exciting trip after we arrived at the camp. We got our rooms in which three girls and three boys were allocated to share the enclosure respectively when we entered our room, I heard my roommates laugh, and their excitement filled with giggles; they were looking extremely impatient for the night because they both had something planned with their boyfriends at midnight. Seema and Naina, my roommates, have asked me if I am seeing Rohan. When Rohan's name came up, I laughed. I told them it is nothing like that, he is only my friend, if anyone of you is interested in him, please take him. But they both looked at me like I was covering my secret affair with Rohan. I opened my mouth to tell them my preference, but I said nothing and kept my mouth shut.

All the girls looked gorgeous as dolls in their short dresses with makeup for the evening atmosphere. And all the boys were handsome and decent in their friendly, laid-back forms. For a change, even Rohan was not looking bad in my eyes.

Many couples were secretly seeing each other in my classroom, and somewhere I was looking for someone special to share my life with. But simultaneously, I was aware that I had to keep patience. Rohan came over and offered me a dance. I saw all the couples getting lost on the dance floor with their partners. I smiled and accepted Rohan's invitation to dance with him. While dancing, Rohan complimented me by saying I looked great in my red dress. I smiled and praised him, too, as he looked very handsome from his regular days. While dancing, DJ changed the Bollywood disco music into slow jazz. I did not want to continue the dance on that slow jazz somewhere, maybe because I was uncomfortable with the closeness while dancing to that music, but Rohan insisted while making a puppy face. I found him cute, and I said OKAY. Rohan drew me closer to him, where I felt his strong hands close to my waist and a firm grasp on other indicators. I avoided him, so I distracted myself by looking left and right at other couples. The romantic ambience lost all the teams in each other arms, and I was feeling somewhere looking like an 'idiot.' Rohan's eyes fixed on me, and I could feel his hot breath on my neck. Once the music ended, I immediately pushed myself and thanked Rohan for the time and the dance. Rohan wanted to tell me something, but I could not hear anything because of the student's noise of loud cheers and whistles. I made a gesture that I could not hear, and with my motion, I said I would return to my room. I waved him bye and left the place. I was exhausted because I wanted to get out of that girlie outfit and be comfortable in my pyjamas and shirt. Seema and Naina were unseen, and there was no chance of returning to the room so soon. When I unzipped my dress, I got a message on my phone from Rohan. He texted me to meet him near the swimming area NOW. The word 'now' raised my eyebrow in many doubts; I was hoping everything was fine with him or what had happened; why did he need me there? Is he okay? Being his friend, I fastened back my dress and rushed to the pool. It was foggy and cold, and I had forgotten to wear the jacket. I found him standing underneath the tree when I got to the swimming area. I asked him why he called me into this silent zone.

Rohan looked at me and hugged me tightly; first, I got startled, but then I felt warm. I was unable to understand why Rohan was acting strangely. I drifted away from him and asked him what the problem was? He smiled and said that he had fallen in love with me from the very beginning. He always searched for the best moment to propose to me, and today, in this beautiful place, after a close dance, this is the best moment to express his feelings for me. I had lost my voice after hearing Rohan's expression of love for me. I was trying to figure out how to explain to Rohan about me. And even if I succeed in explaining, there is little chance he will understand. It was apparent to understand from Rohan's eyes and smile that he was waiting for my big yes. I told Rohan that I had never thought about it, and so far, my priority is my studies and career. I used the term *education* and *career* as an excuse to overcome complicated situations. Rohan was willing to wait for me. He was in no hurry, even though he was expecting the same thing, but he wanted me to be a part of his life as love. Again, I tried to explain to Rohan it was impossible because I didn't love him. Rohan's expression changed after hearing this, and I realised it was too rude to say directly. So immediately, I tried to cover up with the words I meant. I closed my eyes, took a long sigh, and then told him,

"Look, Rohan, I like you just as a friend, no more than that."

"Are you dating someone?" Rohan asked me earnestly.

In a big tone, I yelled, "Noooo!"

"Then what is the issue?" Very frustratingly, Rohan asked me.

I was losing patience as well. Finally, I just said goodbye and started walking because it was pointless to explain further. Rohan came and stood in front of me, and without losing a second, he grabbed me and kissed me hard. It wasn't a kiss. It was sort of an assault on me. I was shocked at this kind of behaviour because I had never imagined this kind of thing, especially from Rohan. I tried to push back Rohan, but his kissing strength was too muscular for me. One way or the other, I slapped him hard and looked at him in shock; he smiled and said, 'I love you."

That is when I lost it all. I burst out of rage; when I saw Rohan smiling at his shameless act. I lost all control over my words and temper. I wish I had used my mental strength instead of power; I came forward and slapped Rohan's face severely.

I grabbed his collar angrily and shouted from my lungs, HOW DARE YOU KISS ME? I DON'T LOVE YOU, ROHAN. I DON'T LIKE MEN. I AM INTO GIRLS; I . . . AM . . . LESBIAN. DID YOU HEAR ME? I AM LESBIAN"

I could only hear my last words, what I had said so plainly; so far, I had never spoken to anyone about my secret. I had even never told myself I was a lesbian. It shocked me too much to hear those words coming out of my mouth.

The moment had come for Rohan to become struck. He stood utterly frozen. And in that tension, another tsunami of shock stood before my eyes. Someone turned on the pool light, and our classmates were under the impact with colourful ribbons and flowers in their hands. It was Rohan's plan, and he wanted to propose to me in front of our friends and make sure we cherished time forever. When I looked around, all I saw were shocked faces. Naina, Seema and a lot of other girls were standing in revelation. There was no voice from anybody; everybody's silence was killing that moment. Everyone started to leave the pool area; only Rohan and I were standing dumb and looking at the pool.

Finally, Rohan looked up at me and said one word, "Sorry."

The moment he said that word, he also left me alone. I was alone, standing in the dark and observing the calmness of the pool for how long, I don't even know that. I cried aloud, never wanting to reveal myself to anyone. I was happy for what I was because that's how God made me. And I had accepted myself gracefully for several years. As a lesbian, I had never been with any girl because

I knew that only a lesbian like me would understand my emotions, not a typical social girl.

After spending a few minutes beside the pool, I returned to my room. When I entered my room, I did not find Seema and Naina; the room was vacant; they had already left the room with their bags and moved to another room. They were uncomfortable about sharing space with a lesbian. I was not surprised by the actions they took. That is why I never told anyone about myself. Rather than understanding me, the girls started treating me as a taboo. The night was too heavy on my head, so I dozed off on the bed without changing.

The following day, I awoke with a burst of laughter outside the lobby. I looked through my window; all my friends had gathered to have breakfast. Everyone was supposed to leave in a short while. I immediately took a shower, got ready with my bag, and went for breakfast. The morning was beautiful, but the memories of the last night were awful. When I entered the dining room, the sound of forks, knives and noisy chitchat turned into silence. I understood that the episode of the night before had spread like a fire. During my breakfast, I felt all eyes on my back. Ignoring everyone, I grabbed my plate and searched for a place to sit. Finally, I found someplace close to the window.

The girls moved out of that zone as soon as I took my place. Nobody wanted to speak with me. I did not look anywhere for any more embarrassment. After I had sipped my coffee, I took my bag and went ahead to sit on the bus; when I entered the bus, there was only one front seat behind the driver, left vacant for me or deliberately left empty. I saw Rohan; he got on the bus, went behind, and did not even look at me. I knew I hurt Rohan's feelings by hiding my biggest truth from him. If I had told him earlier, he would not be giving me his heart. Things would not have messed up, and I would not have shattered his heart of love in front of every classmate. The entire trip was incredibly dull and sad for me. I had never felt bad when the first time I discovered the truth about myself, but my friends' ignorance deeply touched me. Tears flowed down my cheeks because everything had ended for me; all the girls wanted to stay away from me, and the boys did not want to look at me. Rohan's attitude, too, changed towards me. That attentive Rohan had disappeared somewhere in my life.

After I arrived home, there was another shock for me waiting; my dad received a call from the college about me. They spoke about me very accurately. I was entirely unprepared for that. That day, I understood that negativity propagated faster than positivity.

My mother was in tears, and my dad was looking incredibly sad. After that, things get more complicated, especially when you must admit something in front of your parents. It was the first time I ever gave a brave confession. My mother's sobs were heard loud and clear after hearing my confession. Then, finally, I was able to comprehend her feelings. They always talked to me about self-respect and dignity throughout my life and always expected the same from me. But now, I had bought shame on my family. I told my mom that being a lesbian does not mean I have sex with many girls; it has other aspects too. I am lesbian and do not like boys around me; that is it. I want to hang out with girls, and I like girls. But I guess the person who defined lesbianism placed emphasis on sex rather than on explaining feelings. I tried my best to make them understand, but I realized there was no point in talking more when I looked at their sad faces and teary eyes.

I went unobtrusively to my room to check some emails. I found an email from an anonymous asking me questions about how do I satisfy my physical needs? Well, it was clear that this mail was from my class, who did not have the guts to speak on my face. I never felt as bad how much I was feeling then. I wish God had not made me like this; it is not easy to stay regular in this world with ordinary people. I lost my friendship, companionship, and my parent's trust too. I wish I could explain to my parents that I had not betrayed them. All the anger and frustrations had gotten so heavy on my heart that I began to cry aloud as there was nothing I could do. I felt helpless and weirded

Hearing my loud sobs, my parents entered my room; my mother immediately held me and tried to comfort me. My father kept his hand on my head to lift my spirits. When I calmed down, I was astounded by my father's words. He told me they were not upset about knowing the truth about their daughter; what annoyed them was that their daughter's reality came from someone else. They would have felt prouder if I had told them my feelings earlier. However, being a lesbian, the relationship had not changed. I am still their daughter, and I will always be.

Somewhere my parents blame themselves, too; they feel that I had turned into a lesbian because of their conservative thoughts.

If they had been open-minded and allowed me to be friends with boys as a child, I would not have grown up that way. I do not know who is supposed to be responsible? Being a lesbian, I am not taboo to anybody; I have my own choices, way of thinking, and preferences. If I am a lesbian, it does not mean I will tell the girls around to have sex with me. There is nothing to feel insecure or scared about with lesbians. We are too human-like; being lesbian, we are not afraid of other typical genres, so why do normal humans not feel safe or look at us differently.

Society needs to change and give equal respect and rights to lesbians, gay people, and transgender. Please do not hurt their feelings with your sharp words, weird jokes, or ignorance. We are not taboos; your thoughts and your wicked deeds are taboo. We, too, have dreams and ambitions; we were born like that. Is it our fault? If we are born this way, what stands for our survival? Do we have no right to dream or to enlighten our future? We are more robust than ordinary people because we survive in this challenging world. All lesbians, gays and transgender have dignity, and everyone in society should respect them, too.

A NOTE OF THANKS . . .

After SIZZLING WITH NEXT Vol.1, I felt I lacked more. Perhaps authorship is always looking for something new for my readers.

I will start with my handful of readers/reviewers who love to read and review my book. Thank you for being humble and for sharing valuable time with me.

My Husband, **RASHAD KAZI**, without your encouragement and strong faith in me, this second book of erotic would not be possible. You have always served as my light in my darkness. You never doubted my abilities for one moment, even though I doubted my work many times. Thank you, Rashad, for being the strongest pillar of my life.

My deceased parents, NAJMA KAZI and SHAUKAT KAZI, to be forever with me in my heart. With every edition of my book, I miss you very much. One day, we shall meet again.

And 'Thank you' to the lovely people of the EVINCEPUB team for tolerating me and taking the time to answer my questions, Oh-so lame! I know I can be a bug at times.

Thank you, **MR. VIKRAM SINGH THAKUR**, for having accepted the idea of the lesbian erotic genre and with confidence and audacity, you have transformed the few pieces of the manuscript into a beautiful book.

SHAHEEN KAZI

What's
Next?

If you have a moment, please post a brief review on Amazon or GoodReads. Even just a few sentences will help other readers find and enjoy this book as much as you hopefully did.

- Shaheen Kazi

Read more by Shaheen Kazi

Romance

Poems

Horror

Children

If you have a moment, please post a brief review on Amazon or GoodReads. Even a few sentences will help other readers find and enjoy this book as much as you hopefully did.